"You'll have to be careful," Paul warned her

"Daniel Geshard is going to pull out all the stops now to make sure he gets you to back down."

"I'm not the kind of person who is easily persuaded to change her mind once she's made it up," Christa told him shortly.

"You're a woman, though," he retorted, "and by the looks of him, he's the kind of man who thinks he can persuade and seduce a woman into changing her mind— her principles."

"Well, if that's the case, he'll be wasting his time with me—I am not so easily persuadable, and certainly not seducible!"

Let him just dare to try it—let him just dare.

PENNY JORDAN was constantly in trouble in school because of her inability to stop daydreaming—especially during French lessons. In her teens, she was an avid romance reader, although it didn't occur to her to try writing one herself until she was older. "My first half-dozen attempts ended up ingloriously," she remembers, "but I persevered, and one manuscript was finished." She plucked up the courage to send it to a publisher, convinced her book would be rejected. It wasn't, and the rest is history! Penny is married and lives in Cheshire.

Penny Jordan's striking mainstream novel *Power Play* quickly became a *New York Times* bestseller. She followed that success with *Silver, The Hidden Years, Lingering Shadows, For Better For Worse, Cruel Legacy* and, her latest, *Power Games*.

"Women everywhere will find pieces of themselves in Jordan's characters."
—*Publishers Weekly* on *For Better For Worse*

Books by Penny Jordan

HARLEQUIN PRESENTS
1734—TUG OF LOVE
1746—PASSIONATE POSSESSION
1756—PAST LOVING
1774—YESTERDAY'S ECHOES
1805—AN UNFORGETTABLE MAN
1821—UNWANTED WEDDING

THE TRUSTING GAME

Harlequin Books

TORONTO • NEW YORK • LONDON
AMSTERDAM • PARIS • SYDNEY • HAMBURG
STOCKHOLM • ATHENS • TOKYO • MILAN
MADRID • WARSAW • BUDAPEST • AUCKLAND

ISBN 0-373-11839-2

THE TRUSTING GAME

First North American Publication 1996.

Copyright © 1995 by Penny Jordan.

This edition published by arrangement with Harlequin Books S.A.

Printed in U.S.A.

CHAPTER ONE

GRIMACING at the rain, Christa Bellingham hurried from the car park to the hotel forecourt, cursing the abrupt and unforecast change in the weather which meant that she had neither coat nor umbrella to protect her from the heavy downpour.

Up ahead of her a taxi was disgorging its two male passengers into the protection of the canopy above the hotel entrance as Christa ducked her head against the driving rain, mentally bewailing the vanity which had led to her deciding to wear her precious Armani. She was only calling in at the hotel to drop off some fabric samples and prices for John Richards, the hotel manager, on her way to the local Chamber of Commerce, where a talk was being given later in the evening on a subject in which she took a deep and antagonistic interest.

She had protested against the speaker's being invited to address them right from the start, but Howard Findley, the new head of the chamber, had insisted that it was time they shed their old-fashioned stick-in-the-mud image and open themselves up to the possibilities of new theories and projects.

'We might as well give a blank cheque to every charlatan who wants to come and cry his wares and get paid for it,' Christa had protested bitterly.

'Daniel Geshard doesn't charge a speaker's fee,' John had told her mildly, but Christa had refused to be mollified. No matter how much John might have been impressed by the man, Christa knew exactly what type he was—and what he was up to. Deception was the name of the game for men like him, and they didn't care how much pain or suffering they caused in achieving their ends, as she knew all too well... All too well.

Daniel Geshard was coming to talk to them for one purpose and one purpose only—so that he could sell himself and his spurious New Age theories to anyone gullible enough to buy them, and that included the council.

Her head full of angry thoughts, Christa closed her eyes briefly in despair. Howard Findley was a nice man, genuine and good-hearted, but he was no match for the likes of the Daniel Geshards of this world, and already, just on the strength of a telephone chat with the man, Howard was talking enthusiastically about persuading the council to fund several groups of key employees and officials through one of Daniel Geshard's miracle courses.

'He's got this wonderful idea about being able to reach out to even the most disaffected members of our society and to help them get back in touch with themselves, with their real emotions and motivations,' he had enthused. Howard talked like that. Christa much preferred the plain straight facts and realities of life, rather than having them wrapped up in fancy words and theories...

'Whoops!'

The amused male warning and the shock of her totally unexpected contact with the hard, warm body attached to it brought Christa's head up sharply and her mind back to the present. The automatic brisk apology she had been about to give died on her lips as she found herself staring dazedly into a pair of pale grey, thickly lashed male eyes alight with warmth... warmth and something much... much more personal.

Yes. There was a lot more than mere good humour in the way their owner was studying her, just as there was a lot more than mere male good looks in the face they belonged to, Christa admitted as she suddenly found herself struggling slightly for breath while her heart flipped over inside her chest and her pulse-rate beat out an excited tattoo message of approval and attraction.

And he was attractive, Christa recognised, as she stood there half mesmerised, the pouring rain forgotten in her bemused concentration on the man standing in front of her. Tall and powerfully built, almost athletically so, if the speed and skill with which he had so adroitly prevented her from running full-tilt into him was anything to go by, with thick, dark, well-groomed hair and skin that smelled of fresh air and rain rather than some cloying, unpleasantly heavy aftershave.

The dark business suit was fashioned, Christa recognised with an expert eye, out of extremely good cloth and tailored here in this country, which meant that the slightly battered basic Rolex watch he was wearing had probably got that way through constant use on his part rather than being bought second-hand as the latest status-symbol fashion accessory.

This was not a man who needed to underline his masculinity with status symbols of any kind, Christa decided approvingly. This was a man who would have looked equally impressive in an old, worn pair of jeans—equally impressive and very, very male.

Just for a second her mouth curled upwards in delicious feminine fantasy as she momentarily exchanged his suit for those jeans and their present surroundings for a certain TV advertisement made very popular with female viewers by the actor Nick Kamen. As she smiled, the expression in the grey male eyes deepened slightly, intensifying as though he too was conscious of her physical attraction towards him—and shared it.

The strong physical and emotional pull she could feel was so completely unfamiliar to her that it had taken her completely off guard. She felt as though she had somehow stepped into a special and magical world, encompassed by his smile and the warm aura he had thrown almost protectively around her.

As he continued to watch her, the temptation to do something totally out of character and dangerously reckless almost had her taking that small but oh, so giveaway step towards him which he seemed to be silently encouraging and inviting; but then, from the hotel doorway, she heard the man with him calling out impatiently, 'Come on, Daniel, let's get booked in and then I'll go and scout around the town and see if I can find two pretty and willing girls for us to enjoy ourselves with after this talk of yours is over and done with. You'll be ready for a bit of light relief by then, and besides, I need a drink...'

'I'll be with you in a second, Dai.'

Daniel... Christa felt her whole body turn to ice as she stared at the man in front of her in sick disbelief.

'What is it—what's wrong?' he was asking her in apparent concern, taking that small step towards her himself now and, in doing so, narrowing the distance between them to one of close intimacy, the distance of lovers... of seducers.

Daniel. Christa's throat felt as though it had been scraped raw with sandpaper and then doused with acid.

'That wouldn't be Daniel Geshard, would it?' she asked him grittily, her hands balling into small, tight fists.

He was frowning now, his expression puzzled. 'Yes, as a matter of fact it would. But...'

Christa didn't wait to hear any more. Her face flushing with anger and mortification, she immediately stepped away from him, ignoring the hand he was reaching out to detain her, her voice icy with distaste and harsh with angry disgust.

'Is that normally how you see your business meetings, Mr Geshard...as a boring preliminary to the real enjoyment? Hadn't you better go?' she added pointedly. 'Your friend appears to be getting impatient.'

Before he could say anything to her, she turned on her heel and left. John would have to wait for his samples and his quotes. If she followed Daniel Geshard into the hotel foyer now, there was no way she could trust herself not to tell him exactly what she thought of him and all men of his type.

But as she hurried back to her car it wasn't just anger she could feel. So much for her belief in her ability to judge someone's character! How could she have been so stupid? Why hadn't she guessed who he was...what type he was? How could she have been so gullible...she of all people?

Seething inwardly, she got into her car and drove home. She had just enough time to change out of her now damp clothes before the Chamber of Commerce meeting began. There was no way she was going to miss attending it now...no way she intended not to make quite plain her views, her views on the subject of Daniel Geshard's speech... And on the speaker himself?

As soon as she got home, Christa dialled the number of the hotel and explained to the manager that she had been unable to call with his samples but that she would drop them off another time. Then she hurried into her bedroom, where she stripped off her clothes, grimacing in distaste at their clamminess; then she quickly dried and rebrushed her long, thick chestnut hair, confining it with a simple headband after she had put on fresh clothes.

Small and curvaceous, with widely spaced, almost aquamarine-coloured eyes in a pretty heart-shaped face, Christa had had to work hard to banish other people's image of her as a pretty woman with no real head for business. Firmly refusing to compromise or alter the way she looked, or make herself conform to a stereotypical and often male idea of what a businesswoman should look like, hadn't always been easy, especially in the early days when she had taken over the business from her great-aunt. She knew that there were still those locally who thought she had fallen on her feet in inheriting her aunt's textile import business, but in the years before her death her great-aunt had let the business become very run-down.

Christa had been brought up by her great-aunt after her own parents' deaths, and before going to university and training as a designer she had frequently travelled abroad with her relative, visiting the various suppliers from whom she bought her cloth.

It had been cheaper and more practical for the older woman to take her great-niece with her during the school holidays, rather than try to find someone else to look after her, and out of loyalty and love for her great-aunt Christa had kept silent about the way in which she had lost her grip on the business.

It had saddened Christa to discover how much her great-aunt had lost her old skills of running ahead of the market and picking the right fabrics, and to see how some of her suppliers had started to fob her off with inferior cloths.

Christa had had to work hard to reverse all that. Sometimes she had had to behave more ruthlessly than was really in her nature to do, but at least the business was beginning to pick up again. Her training and flair as a designer had helped her, of course, and the bank manager was just beginning to stop frowning every time he saw her.

'You're so damned self-possessed,' a would-be boy-friend had once complained to her. 'Sometimes I wonder just what the hell it would take to break down that barrier of yours. Whatever it is, whoever it is, it isn't me... What is it you're waiting for, Christa?' he had demanded angrily. 'A prince?'

'I'm not waiting for anyone... any man,' Christa had told him truthfully.

And yet earlier this evening, just for a moment... Angrily she picked up her jacket.

Thank God she had realised just who Daniel Geshard was before... before what?

Nothing would really have happened. She just mustn't allow her feelings, her emotions, however powerful they might be, to control her. She had seen all too clearly the disastrous consequences that could result from a woman believing she was in love and loved in turn by the kind of man who earned his living through deceit... Like Piers Philips.

Quickly she closed her eyes. Even now, after all these years, it still hurt her to think of Laura. To remember...

She and Laura had been at university together, and they had both been in their final year when Laura had met and fallen for Piers Philips, a New Age self-acclaimed philosopher and guru with whom Laura had become so besotted that she had dropped out of the course before taking her finals and married him.

Laura's father was an extremely wealthy industrialist, and Laura herself had inherited a considerable amount of money from her grandmother. She and Piers intended to use this, she told Christa enthusiastically, to buy a large country house where Piers would open a counselling and stress clinic.

Christa had to admit that even she had been taken in by Piers' enthusiasm and ideals. She had been so very gullible and innocent then, even half envying Laura her charismatic husband and the wonderful life they were going to build together.

But, once Laura and Piers were married, things very quickly started to go wrong. Laura complained then that she suspected that Piers was being unfaithful to her; that he neglected her.

Christa would never forgive herself for the fact that she had allowed Piers to convince her Laura was suffering from some kind of hormonal depression brought on by her pregnancy, and that the affair she was accusing him of was completely imaginary, so that, instead of supporting Laura, she had urged her to put aside her doubts and concentrate on the future, to think of her marriage and her coming baby.

Piers had taken her out to dinner to thank her for her support. 'Laura couldn't have a better friend,' he had told her.

A better friend... Christa's throat tightened in remembered grief and pain.

The only excuse she could give herself was that she had been young and naïve and that, even then, Piers had been an arch manipulator, enjoying the game he was playing with both of them, enjoying deceiving them.

Three months after their baby, a little girl, was born, Piers had left Laura amid a storm of gossip. The girl he had left Laura for came from an aristocratic and very rich family. Laura's money, the money she had inherited from her grandmother, had all gone; all she had had left was the mountain of debts Piers had run out on.

'Some of his clients have even threatened to sue for malpractice,' Laura had sobbed when Christa had tried to comfort her.

'You'll get over him,' Christa had told her comfortingly.

'No, I won't... I'll never get over him,' Laura had told her bleakly. 'How can I?'

Six weeks later she was dead. An overdose taken while she was in the grip of post-natal depression had been the official verdict, but Christa suspected otherwise... It was her relationship with Piers, and his systematic and cold-hearted deceit of her, that had killed her, she was sure, and Christa had vowed that never, ever again would she allow herself, or anyone else, to be taken in by that kind of man; she would do everything and anything she could to reveal and to expose what they really were.

As she intended to do this evening with Daniel Geshard.

She looked at herself bleakly in the mirror before she went downstairs. It had shocked and disturbed her that she would have so easily fallen victim to his apparent charm. Was she in some way particularly flawed, in that she seemed destined not to be immediately able to recognise his type? Well, Daniel Geshard was one con-man she was not going to be taken in by, and she intended to make sure that he knew it.

* * *

'And now, on behalf of us all, I would just like to thank our speaker for his most informative and...'

Informative rubbish. Christa fumed; everything she had heard tonight only confirmed and strengthened her belief that the kind of role-changing games advocated by this supposed guru of the latest business fad were, in real business terms, completely worthless.

And as for the speaker himself... anger deepened the warm peach-coloured skin of Christa's face as she contemplated the man standing behind the podium with glittering aquamarine eyes.

For some reason she had anticipated that Daniel Geshard, their speaker, would have cultivated a slightly more green and politically correct appearance, choosing to wear, instead of his immaculate suit—a suit which she had already observed at close hand and knew to be extremely expensive—something more disarming and 'friendly'... battered cords, perhaps, and a thick hand-knitted sweater... or jeans and...

No, not the fantasy of the jeans again! The angry glitter of her eyes became even more pronounced, the self-derisory curl of her mouth even stronger, and she reflected on her own idiotic folly in actually imagining that she could possibly have found such a man physically attractive, that her heart had actually skipped that betraying beat, that she had actually felt that small dangerous thrill of sensual excitement.

He was a poseur, a charlatan... a con-man bent on coaxing the foolish and unwary to part with their money in return for some unsubstantiated and unsubstantiatable claim that he could somehow turn their supposedly tired and stressed employees into people with so much enthusiasm for their work that they would doubtless enable their employers to recoup the cost of sending them on his courses by their astonishing diligence and delight in their work.

No. The only person to profit from what he claimed he had to offer would be him, Christa decided contemptuously.

The head of the Chamber of Commerce was asking if anyone wanted to ask any questions.

Immediately, Christa got to her feet.

The manufactured pleasure in Daniel Geshard's grey eyes as they studied her made her lip curl in disdain. Oh, yes, she had seen the way he had reacted when he'd spotted her in his audience, the quick, oh, so false smile of warm pleasure—followed by a small questioning frown as she turned her head away, refusing to acknowledge his recognition of her.

But then, of course, it was in his interests to deceive her into believing that he found her attractive. Grimly she wondered how many female executives had succumbed to that heart-twisting grey-eyed message of interest and attraction, only to discover that what he really wanted was their signature on a form enticing their employees to take part in one of his ridiculous courses.

'Er—yes, Christa...?'

She could hear the chairman clearing his throat nervously as he acknowledged her intention to speak. Unlike her foe, he would, of course, know exactly what was coming. She had never made any secret of her views when the subject of inviting this man to speak to them had first been mooted.

And nor, she reassured herself firmly, did her intention to demolish the very smooth and polished persuasiveness he had just used to attempt to sell them his New Age theories have anything to do with her personal feelings about him as a man—nor with her potentially humiliating misreading of his body-language and the look of warm male interest she had mistakenly thought she'd seen in his eyes when she had not known his identity.

Fortunately, she had discovered who he was in time!

No matter what other people's views might be, she was not taken in by his pseudo-psychological expertise—she knew a fake when she saw one.

What real proof had he offered them, after all, that this centre he owned and ran in the Welsh mountains really benefited the people who attended his courses?

'What I would like to ask the Chair is what actual proof Mr Geshard can offer us that his courses, his centre do improve the profitability of the companies sending their executives to him.'

He was a good actor, Christa acknowledged grimly, as his expression betrayed neither discomfort nor surprise at her question.

'Very little.'

His prompt 'very little' made Christa's eyebrows snap together in amazement.

'You don't feel there is any need to keep such records, then?' she questioned him mock sweetly. 'Unusual, especially in an age where even the most obvious of fake wonder-cures insist on producing reality-defying "before and after" test results.'

Although she had not taken her eyes off his face, Christa was still aware of the faint ripple of disapproval that ran through the chamber. Disapproval which she knew was directed at her and not the speaker—but then she was not a man, was she, not part of the unofficial 'club' which ran such organisations?

'Perhaps, but since we've only been open less than a year, and since none of the companies who have used our services has yet produced a full year's accounts, we do not as yet have access to such figures. However, it seems as though I may have inadvertently given the wrong impression with my speech. Our aim is not specifically to increase our client's profits, but rather to improve and enhance the quality of their employees' lives, both at work and away from it.'

'By forcing them to play games?' Christa demanded, maintaining eye-contact with him.

'It's a well-known and accepted fact now that children who are deprived of the opportunity for play are far more likely to grow into maladjusted adults. What we are about is teaching people to work harmoniously together, teaching them how to combat the stresses of modern living.'

'But you admit that you cannot back up your claims with hard facts,' Christa persisted doggedly, refusing to be quelled by the cool grey-eyed stare he was giving her, so very different from the warm male interest with which he had regarded her earlier that day—correction: the warm male interest with which she had *thought* he had regarded her; just like his claims this evening, that warmth, that interest had been completely spurious.

'Was it an admission? I rather thought I was merely correcting your—er—inaccurate interpretation of my speech.'

The male laughter which greeted his comment made Christa's face burn, but she wasn't going to be bullied into backing down, and she certainly wasn't going to be stupid enough to fall for that false look of brief sympathy which had flashed in his eyes.

'You have no real proof that what you are doing, the courses you offer, have any kind of genuine benefit, other than to *your* cash-flow.'

Now she had got under his skin, she realised triumphantly as she saw the way his mouth and eyes hardened.

'Not perhaps in balance-sheet terms—either my own or anyone else's—but *I* certainly believe in the benefits of what we are doing, and I can tell you this: if you were to undergo one of our courses yourself, I promise you it would completely change the way you view your life.'

His voice had dropped slightly as he spoke and for some reason Christa felt her face start to burn again, her thoughts winging back to that small, betraying moment that afternoon when he had looked at her, and yet she had been drawn towards him, the deepest feminine core of her instinctively responding to him and to the message he had seemed to be giving to her.

When her heartbeat accelerated now, though, it was with anger and not attraction, her eyes darkening as she challenged him. 'Impossible.'

'On the contrary, I can categorically promise you and everyone else here that after, say, a month at the centre, your views on life, the focus of your life will have changed—and I'll go even further. I'll add that you yourself will be happy to admit to those changes, to acknowledge them and want to share them with others . . .'

'Never!' Christa denied.

'Let me prove it to you.'

Christa opened her mouth to vehemently refuse his challenge and then realised abruptly that she had backed herself into a very imprisoning corner.

'I think that's a very generous offer, and an excellent idea,' the chairman was saying warmly to the audience, taking advantage of Christa's momentary silence. 'We shall all be most interested to see the results of Christa's visit to your centre . . .'

'No, I can't,' Christa started to protest breathlessly. 'My business doesn't generate the kind of profits for——'

'There won't be any charge.'

Christa gulped in air. What had she done? If she refused now, she would not only make herself look a complete idiot, she would also be allowing him to gain the advantage. To win. She could see already how impressed the others were by his confidence, his belief in himself.

'You can't back out now, Christa,' the chairman was warning her jovially, but Christa could see his resentment of her in his eyes. 'Otherwise we'll begin to think that you're the one who doesn't have the courage of her convictions.'

'I had no intention of backing out,' Christa denied stiffly. 'I shall need a week to organise my business affairs,' she told her opponent without looking directly at him.

'Yes, of course...'

How smooth he was...how assured...how confident of victory; but the war wasn't over yet, and it would take more than charm and confidence to change her mind. Much, much more... In fact, Christa decided, recovering slightly from the shock of the way he had turned the tables on her, he was the one who would ultimately lose out, not her, because there was nothing, nothing that he could say or do that would convince her.

'Our speaker outmanoeuvred you very neatly tonight, didn't he?'

Christa frowned, increasing her speed as the man addressing her fell into step beside her. She had never particularly liked Paul Thompson. He had an unctuous, almost oily manner which did nothing to hide the blatant sexual curiosity Christa had seen in his eyes whenever he looked at a woman. She had had to rebuff the heavy-handed attempts at flirting with her on more than one occasion, and, although she had no doubt that he would be quite happy to go to bed with her, she knew that he also resented her, and she suspected that he was one of those men who secretly did not really like women at all.

She felt very sorry for his wife, and avoided him as much as she could.

'You'll have to be careful,' he warned her, mock solicitously. 'Our speaker is going to pull out all the stops now to make sure he gets you to back down. He can't afford to do anything else. Not having gone so public, so to speak.'

'I'm not the kind of person who is easily persuaded to change her mind once she's made it up,' Christa told him shortly. 'You should know that, Paul.'

'You're a woman, though,' he retorted, plainly nettled by her comment, 'and by the looks of him he's the kind of man who...'

'Who what?' Christa demanded acidly.

'The kind of man who thinks he can persuade and seduce a woman into changing her mind...her principles.'

'Well, if that's the case, he'll be wasting his time with me—I'm not so easily persuadable and certainly not seducible!' Perhaps, a small inner voice warned her, but if she had not realised in time just who he was... But she had realised, she reassured herself firmly, and having done so—well, if Daniel Geshard was thinking for one moment along the lines that Paul was so mockingly suggesting, he was going to be in for one hell of a big surprise, she told herself with grim pleasure. Let him just dare to try it—let him just dare.

CHAPTER TWO

CHRISTA frowned as she heard her front doorbell ring. From her attic workroom it was three flights down to the front door of the large Victorian semi which had been her home ever since she had come to live here with her aunt, after her parents' death.

Whoever was ringing her doorbell had no right to be doing so anyway; everyone knew that her working hours were sacrosanct and that she was not to be interrupted.

Her aunt had preferred to work in the small office attached to the warehouse where they stored their cloth, but Christa, with her training as a designer, loved the large north-lit attic-room, where she could work in peace without any interruptions.

Where she could *normally* work in peace without any interruptions, she corrected herself, as the doorbell continued to ring.

Well, she wasn't going to answer it, so whoever was there would just have to go away. Before she left for Wales tonight she wanted to finish the project she was working on. People outside the business always expressed astonishment when they learned how far ahead she worked. The fabric samples she was studying now would not be on the market until the summer season after next, and the design council, along with the fashion industry, were even further ahead, working on the colours and styles that people would be wearing two winters from now.

Designers were obviously much taken with the theme of the new century and of the change in the stellar constellations which would bring in the new age of Aquarius. The samples she was studying now featured all manner of such symbols: stars, suns, moons, along with various interpretations of the sign of Aquarius and its link to water.

The colours, too, reflected that same watery element, blues and greens, highlighted with a range of sand colours from palest beige right through to glittering gold.

Thoughtfully she fingered a piece of deep blue damask, gazing at the neat piles of samples on the table in front of her until she found what she was looking for. The old-gold brocade looked good with the damask— good but slightly dull, she acknowledged, thinking ahead to how the various combinations of the fabrics she would choose would feature in advertising displays. The aqua fabric with the gold suns on it, while not to everyone's taste, provided a dramatic contrast to the two plainer fabrics.

The buyer from the designer shops had been flatteringly complimentary about her present range of fabrics, even if the order he had given her had been smaller than she could have hoped.

'Nice, but very expensive,' had been his comments about one of the damasks she had shown him in rich jewel colours.

'Because of the quality of the fabric,' Christa had told him. 'In ten years' time this fabric will just be starting to develop the elegant shabby patina you see in fabrics in old houses, where something cheaper will merely be wearing away.'

'Mmm . . . In my business we don't always encourage our clients to think long-term,' he had responded drily.

The doorbell had stopped ringing. Christa smiled in satisfaction, and then frowned as it suddenly started to ring again.

Whoever it was was plainly not going to go away.

Thoroughly angry, she put down the samples she had been studying and headed for the stairs.

By the time she reached the front door Christa was not only out of temper, she was out of breath as well. Flipping her hair back off her face, she pushed it out of the way with one hand as she opened the door.

'Look,' she began irritably, 'I'm working and...'

Her voice died away as she gazed in shock at her unexpected visitor.

Daniel Geshard. What was he doing here? Had he come perhaps to tell her that he had changed his mind, that he was withdrawing his challenge to her?

The amusement in his eyes as he studied her didn't seem to suggest that he was a man who had come cap in hand seeking favours, and Christa flushed as she recognised that part of his amusement seemed to be caused by the fact that she was barefoot.

It was a habit of hers to spread her samples on the floor and kick off her shoes when she knelt down to study them. She had never in the past thought of her feet as a particularly provocative part of her body, but now, for some reason, she could feel her face starting to flush as she fought down the urge to curl her toes into the carpet in an effort to conceal them from him.

He looked so much taller than she had remembered, so much more...more male. He was wearing jeans, a warm-looking blue shirt tucked into the waistband, and Christa felt her hot colour deepen slightly as she remembered how she had fantasised about seeing him wearing just such clothing.

Her imagination had not done him justice, she acknowledged unwillingly. No man had any right to have such long legs, such powerful thighs.

She tensed as, without asking her, he edged through the door and into the hallway, affording her a sideways view of his very male profile and his tautly firm... Christa swallowed quickly. Trust him to catch her at such a disadvantage, wearing an old, comfortable top and a pair of leggings, her face free of make-up, her hair loose and all over the place. Where had he got her address from? she wondered as she studied him surreptitiously. He was a very good-looking man, a very virile-looking man, she had to give him that. She shivered slightly, hastily looking... 'What do you want?' she demanded, trying to control the situation again as he paused to study a collage of fabrics she had made while she was at college and which her aunt had proudly insisted on hanging in the hallway.

She should have taken it down, Christa reflected as he withdrew his gaze from her collage and focused it on her.

'What do I want?' he repeated. 'Well...'

Something in the way he was looking at her made Christa feel as though she had unexpectedly stepped on to a patch of sheet ice and found herself dangerously, physically, out of control because of it.

'I meant, what are you doing here?' she corrected herself swiftly.

'Ah.'

A rueful smile curled his mouth. Determinedly, Christa hardened her heart. In any other man his apparent sense of humour would have delighted her, but with this man nothing could be taken at face value, as she already had good cause to know.

It was in his interests, after all, to win her over to his side—part of the softening-up process he undoubtedly intended to use on her to get her to change her mind about his precious centre.

'I've come to collect you,' Christa heard him saying in response to her question. 'The centre isn't that easy to find...'

'To collect me? I'm not a parcel!' she said, adding acidly, 'And in view of the fact that I've so far managed to find my way to some extremely obscure parts of the world, I doubt very much that finding my way to Wales should prove too much of a problem.'

'You do still intend to take the course, then?'

Christa shot him an angry look. Did he honestly think she was going to back out; that she *could* back out?

'Of course I intend to take it,' she confirmed fiercely.

'Good.'

'But the course doesn't start until tomorrow morning at ten and I still have work to finish, so if you will excuse me——' Christa began pointedly.

The dark eyebrows rose. 'The last train from our nearest main-line station to our local one leaves at four in the afternoon. You'll be cutting things pretty fine.'

Train? Christa stared at him.

'I don't intend... I'm not travelling by train; I'm taking my car.'

'Ah...I'm afraid not. People attending our courses are not allowed to bring their own transport,' he told her firmly.

'What? I don't believe it...you...'

'It's in our brochure,' he told her unapologetically. 'I did send you a copy.'

Yes, he had, and she had promptly thrown it away without bothering to read it, so angry had she been at the way she had allowed herself to be manipulated into such a time-wasting situation.

'That's why I thought you might appreciate a lift...'

Suspiciously Christa watched him through narrowed eyes. What was the real purpose of his visit? Not to do her any favours, she was sure of it. If she didn't arrive on time for the commencement of her course, would he gloatingly proclaim that she had backed out of their arrangement and seize this as evidence that she was afraid of losing?

'I can't leave yet,' she told him edgily. 'I'm still working and I haven't packed...'

'That's all right. I can wait...'

Wait... Where? Not here, Christa decided, but he seemed to have other ideas.

He was studying her collage again.

'Nice...' he told her. 'You have an excellent eye for colour, but did you know that your choice of such rich colours, especially the red, denotes a very powerfully driven and ambitious personality?'

'And you, of course, would know about such things,' Christa agreed derisively. 'It goes hand in hand...'

'It *is* one of the subjects I have studied,' he agreed, apparently not picking up on her contempt. At least not on the surface; whatever else might be fake about him, she was pretty sure that his intelligence was genuine enough. Which meant that he was more than likely suppressing what he really felt...because he wanted to lull her into a state of false security. Well, she would soon make him realise his mistake.

'You're wasting your time, you know,' she told him curtly; 'there's absolutely no way that spending a month or even six months in the middle of the Welsh countryside is going to change anything about me or my outlook on life. And besides,' she challenged him, her eyes narrowing watchfully, 'surely I'm right in thinking that the normal duration of such courses would only be two weeks at the most?'

He looked, Christa recognised in swift triumph, almost uncomfortable—uncomfortable and rather caught off balance by her question, although he quickly hid it, turning his head slightly away from her so that she couldn't see his full expression. Was that *just* discomposure she had seen in his eyes or had there been a hint of anger there as well? she wondered gleefully. If she had managed to get under his skin already, then so much the better. She was not afraid of his anger—she welcomed it. When people lost control of their emotions they betrayed themselves more easily.

'Normally, yes,' she heard him agreeing, 'but in your case...'

'You decided to balance the scales in your own favour and give yourself extra time,' she suggested tauntingly.

To her surprise he didn't try to deny her accusation or to defend himself, instead giving her a look that for some unaccountable reason made her pulse start to race frantically and her heart to execute a high-dive.

'It's no good,' she repeated quickly, 'I shan't change my mind...'

The long, level look he gave her rather surprised her. That he should acknowledge her antagonism was to be expected, but that he should allow her to see that it affected him wasn't. Men like him were very much into control of their own emotions as well as those of the people around them. She would have expected him to want to give her the impression that he was above acknowledging her dislike, not to react to it with such a very male and challenging gleam in those cool, grey eyes... The kind of gleam that, if she was foolish enough to be vulnerable to his particular brand of male magnetism, could quite easily have made her heart beat just a little faster and her body...

'You sound very sure about that.'

The gleam was gone now, replaced by a cool, distancing scrutiny. 'I am,' Christa confirmed firmly. 'I know myself very well.'

'Yourself, or the self you allow yourself to be? You do realise how stressful such rigid control of your personality is, don't you?'

Christa glared angrily at him.

'And you would know about such things, I take it. Tell me...what exactly did you do before you jumped on the modern bandwagon of the...the quasi-professional soothsayer and reader of runes?' Christa demanded insultingly.

She waited for the storm to break, for the grey eyes to darken and the sensually curved male mouth to utter retaliatory insults, but to her consternation he said simply instead, 'I lectured in psychology at Oxford. I don't want to rush you, but it would be a good idea if we could leave pretty soon. I don't want to get back too much after dark. We haven't had much wind recently, and if the power supply is low it might mean starting up our subsidiary generator...'

The speed with which he changed subjects, the apparent calmness in his manner after delivering a statement which had left her feeling as flattened as though she had been mown down by a boulder, left Christa floundering and impotently angry, not just with him but with herself as well.

A lecturer in psychology...

'It was in the brochure, along with the qualifications of the other members of our staff.'

The quiet statement brought a surge of humiliated colour to Christa's skin, despite her attempts to stop it.

'A generator,' she repeated, determinedly adopting his own tactics. 'Does that mean you don't have a proper reliable electricity supply?'

'We aren't on the national grid, no,' he agreed. 'Our electricity is generated by wind machines. We try at the centre to be as environmentally aware and as independent as possible. That includes generating our own electricity, growing our own fruit and vegetables. We even tried supplying our own meat, but that didn't work out too well.

'The sheep became too tame and no one wanted to send them to market,' he explained. 'Same with the hens; none of us could bring ourselves to wring their necks.'

Mentally, Christa contrasted what he was saying with the lives of some of the people in the villages she had visited in India and Pakistan. There they did not have the luxury of allowing their livestock to become tame pets.

As though he had read her mind, he said quietly, 'Yes, I know what you're thinking and you're probably right, but would you have wanted to be the one to sign the death warrant?'

His perception was beginning to disconcert her.

'It would depend whose name was on it,' she told him pithily.

The sound of his laughter surprised and irked her. He was supposed to get offended, angry, to be betrayed by his pride and ego into revealing himself as he really was— not to be tolerantly amused.

Daniel Geshard was dangerous, Christa acknowledged uneasily. His claim that a month on one of his
courses would change her entire outlook on life was one
she still scathingly discounted. Her own claim to herself
that, knowing who he was, or more importantly what
he was, there was not the slightest risk of that initial tug
of empathy and attraction she had felt towards him being
rekindled—*that* claim was the truth, wasn't it?

'What's wrong?'

Christa tensed against his choice of words—not the
impersonal, 'Is something wrong?' but the much, much
more personal, 'What's wrong?' as though he already
knew her so well that it was taken for granted that he
knew that something was.

'What's wrong?' She gave him a cold stare.
'Nothing's wrong,' she told him bitingly, 'apart from
the fact that you've interrupted me in the middle of some
important work, practically forced your way into my
home, tried to take total control of my life...'

'The decision to accept my offer was yours,' he pointed
out easily. 'You could always have refused.'

Liar, Christa wanted to say. He knew damn well she
could not have refused it without totally losing face. As
she turned her back to walk away from him she heard
him saying to her, 'You'll need to pack at least three
changes of outdoor clothes, plus a warm weatherproof
coat. When we get snow...'

'Snow?' Christa stopped and whirled round. 'It's
October,' she objected derisively. 'We don't *get* snow in
this country in October...'

'Maybe not, but Wales is a different country and we
do get snow, and we're up in the mountains, high enough
to have bad snow as early as September in some years.

'Did you manage to get walking boots, by the way?' Daniel called after her.

'Walking boots?'

'It was on the list of required clothing,' he told her.

And the list had no doubt been with the brochure which she had thrown away, Christa acknowledged hollowly. What else had she omitted to discover through that foolish piece of stiff-necked pride?

'No, I did not manage to get walking boots,' she enunciated grimly. 'But then I shan't need them as I shall not be doing any walking.'

If she had expected him to respond to her challenge by arguing with her she was disappointed... As though she simply hadn't spoken, he continued easily, 'Well, don't worry about it too much. There's an excellent sports and climbing equipment shop in our local market town. You'll like visiting it—everyone does. It's still very much a traditional market town, with a weekly cattle auction. You'll enjoy it...'

Christa gave him a withering look.

'I hardly think so,' she told him dismissively. 'I'm a city person, I'm afraid...' It wasn't really true, but she was beginning to feel not just resentful but, more worryingly, slightly afraid of the way he seemed to be continuously reading her mind, second-guessing her. 'Watching some bucolic farmers haggling over the sale of a handful of ragged sheep is hardly my idea of pleasure...'

'No?' The dark eyebrows rose. 'That isn't what I've heard. Apparently they've learned to be extremely wary of the English cloth-lady in the factories of India and Pakistan.'

Christa tensed warily. Where had he learned that?

'Buying cloth is my job...watching other people buying sheep isn't. Besides, I thought the ethos behind these courses was that one put aside all thoughts of work and learned, instead, to play,' she commented mockingly.

'Our ethos, as you call it, is to teach people, to *help* people to live well-balanced and fulfilling lives; to learn to acknowledge and accept that the human psyche has other needs besides the more material ones.'

'Oh, the trauma of the poor stressed-out executive,' Christa taunted disparagingly. 'How great his need, how noble the role of the one who eases it for him. There's a real world peopled by human beings who are starving...dying...'

'Yes, I do know,' he told her quietly.

There was a certain note in the quiet male voice which for some reason made Christa flush slightly and look away from him, as though she was the one in error...at fault.

'I cannot alleviate the ills of the starving—would that I could—but I can help people to come to terms with themselves, to learn to live in harmony with others. If all the world lived in such harmony,' he told her gently, 'there would be no wars, or famine.

'I'll wait down here for you, shall I?' he continued.

Christa looked at him blankly. His words had caused her to feel such emotion... He baffled and bewildered her, catching her so repeatedly off guard that she felt like a wooden doll on a string which he manipulated.

Careful, she warned herself as she hurried upstairs, you're letting him get to you and you mustn't. Remember what he is, not what he seems to be. He's a psychologist; he knows how people behave, how they react, and he knows how to project a specific image, how to gain someone's sympathy and admiration.

But he would soon learn that she wasn't so easy to deceive, and before her month in Wales was over he would be bitterly regretting his foolish public claim to be able to change her whole outlook on life. God might have wrought such a transformation in St Paul on the road to Damascus, but Daniel Geshard was a mere human being.

A mere human being... She paused, just with one foot on the second flight of stairs, her heart suddenly missing a small beat. There was nothing 'mere' about the man, and she would do well to hang on grimly to that fact.

CHAPTER THREE

'Is THIS it?' Christa asked in dismay at the ramshackle collection of stone-built, low-roofed buildings beyond the closed farm gate.

'This' looked more like a small farmhouse surrounded by farm buildings than a study centre. For starters, from the size of the main building she doubted that it could house more than four or five people.

'Not exactly,' he returned calmly, bringing the Land Rover to a halt in front of the gate.

Christa had been startled at first when she had seen the Land Rover. Somehow she had expected him to drive something more... more expensive... more image-reinforcing... A four-wheel-drive vehicle, certainly, but a top-of-the-range model, not this battered vehicle which looked as though it was held together with bits of string.

As he had watched her studying it, Daniel had told her with visible pride that he had rescued and rebuilt the vehicle himself.

'Yes, it looks like it,' Christa had agreed grimly, and then had felt oddly mean as she saw the pleasure fade from his eyes. Men did have, somewhere within their make-up, that little-boy eagerness and enthusiasm for certain cherished things.

'What do you mean, not exactly?' she asked him suspiciously as he opened the Land Rover door.

'This isn't the centre,' he admitted. 'This is my home... The centre closed down at the end of last month...to

34

give the staff a chance to have a break and to enable the builders to finish work on a new extension.'

'What...you mean you've brought me here under totally false pretences?' Christa flashed. 'Well, in that case you can just turn this...this collection of rusty metal and string around and take me back again.'

'Impossible, I'm afraid,' Daniel told her calmly. 'For one thing, I'm almost out of petrol, and Dai won't be here with a fresh supply for me until some time tomorrow, and for another...it's too late, Christa,' he told her quietly, looking at her, watching her. She recognised a small heart-stopping surge of confused emotion—anger because he had deceived her and relief because he was refusing to let her go?

'You agreed to come here,' he reminded her, repeating his earlier words to her.

'I agreed to attend a course held at your centre, not to...what do you mean, all the staff are having a break?' she questioned him uncertainly.

'Just that,' he told her. 'But you needn't be concerned; I'm quite happy to conduct your course personally,' he assured her. 'In fact,' he told her, his voice taking on a disturbing husky timbre, 'I'm positively looking forward to it...'

'Well, I'm not,' Christa snapped. 'And in fact—— What's that?' she demanded, her eyes rounding with shock as the Land Rover suddenly rocked startlingly from side to side. In her efforts to counteract the rocking effect she reached out instinctively to brace herself against it, one hand pressed against the doorframe, the other...

The other, she recognised, was pressed flat against something much more solid and warm than a doorframe. And that something was Daniel's chest, his heartbeat a steady regular rhythm beneath her hand.

'It's all right.' She heard him laughing. 'It's only Clarence... he's come to welcome us home...'

'Clarence...' Christa stared wildly at him. 'Clarence,' she repeated uncertainly. She couldn't see anyone through the windows of the vehicle.

'He's a billy goat,' Daniel told her, 'who hasn't yet learned that a head-butt is not always exactly an approved mode of welcome.' He was laughing at her, Christa recognised indignantly as she saw the small creases fanning out around his eyes and the humour in the upward curl of his mouth. 'I'm sorry if he frightened you. I should have warned you...'

'I wasn't frightened,' Christa denied untruthfully.

She started to pull away from him and then tensed in shock as one of his hands covered hers, holding it trapped against his chest while his thumb stroked caressingly over the soft skin of her inner wrist.

She could feel herself starting to tremble slightly; the skin of his hands was slightly rough, as though he spent a good deal of time outside, and the small abrasion of it rubbing against her much softer flesh was causing odd shivers of sensation to quiver through her body.

'Liar,' she heard Daniel accusing her softly.

Shaking, she tried to focus on what he was saying to her instead of what was happening inside her.

'Your pulse is fast,' he told her in explanation. 'And a fast pulse means...'

'All right, so it was a shock,' Christa admitted, anxious to bring an end to what was becoming an increasingly hazardous situation. Fear was one cause of a racing pulse, it was true, but there were others. She bit her lip, chagrined by the knowledge that what her body had idiotically interpreted as a small caress had, in fact, been nothing more than a clinical examination of her pulse-rate.

'Whoops, hang on...' The sensation of Daniel's arms suddenly coming round her and holding her wrapped tightly against his chest choked the breath out of her lungs, leaving her totally unable to make any kind of verbal protest as Clarence sent the Land Rover rocking a second time.

'I think he's getting impatient,' she heard Daniel saying somewhere above her head.

She was pressed so firmly against him that to make any comment would have meant risking her lips virtually touching the warm, bare skin of his throat as she tried to speak. In fact, if she opened her mouth at all, it would be almost as though she were doing so in order to kiss him.

'Hey...you're trembling...it's all right, Clarence isn't so fearsome. In fact he's quite a softie once you get to know him... come on.'

Thank goodness he had started to release her and turn away from her to open his door before he could realise that the reason for that small, intense shudder had not been anything to do with Clarence at all, wary though she was of the animal.

What was the matter with her? There was obviously a very large communications gap between her body and her brain; her body was still locked into that first initial meeting between them and the instant attraction she had felt towards him.

It was time that her brain told it very clearly and firmly just what the real situation now was.

'Come and meet Clarence,' Daniel invited, holding open the passenger door for her.

Reluctantly Christa climbed out of the vehicle. It wasn't just the goat that was making her feel on edge, with his impressive set of formidably sharp-looking horns, but the man standing beside him as well.

'I bought him as a kid. Goat's milk is extremely good for you and the plan was that his harem would contribute towards making us self-sufficient.

'Unfortunately things didn't turn out quite as I'd hoped. It's cheaper and easier to buy our milk from the supermarket. It wasn't so much Clarence's and his wives' predilection for breaking out of their pen that caused the trouble as their taste for clothes...

'They ate them,' he explained with a grin when Christa turned her head briefly away from the wary study of the billy goat to him. 'I managed to find homes for his wives but Clarence unfortunately has proved hard to rehouse. Still, he makes a very good guard animal and, unlike a dog, he has to be neither licensed nor muzzled.'

Christa didn't quite like the way the goat was watching her, or her clothes, but she was damned if she was going to admit as much to his owner.

When Daniel turned to walk away from her, calling over his shoulder to her, 'Hang on a sec, I'll just get your case,' Christa had to suppress her desire to betray her weakness and protest.

Clarence returned her determined eye-contact with an unblinking stare that she could have sworn had a faintly taunting element to it. And when the animal suddenly started to move towards her, she had to fight to stop herself from scuttling behind Daniel's protective bulk.

'He'll soon get to know you,' Daniel told her as he reached out to scratch between the animal's ears.

'I can't wait,' Christa muttered sardonically, firmly keeping Daniel's body between her and the goat as they walked towards the house. What on earth had she got herself into? she wondered bitterly as she waited for Daniel to unlock the door. A month cooped up virtually alone with a man who she already knew was a danger to her, and for what? Just so that she could prove a point?

She must be feeling more tired than she had realised, she decided as Daniel pushed open the door and motioned her inside. Her principles and her beliefs had always been very important to her. Her great-aunt had been the old-fashioned type, with very strict and strong values which she had passed on to Christa.

The door opened directly into a large, low-ceilinged kitchen. And as Christa glanced round the room, observing the bright red Aga and the solid cherrywood kitchen units, she reflected cynically that no expense had been spared in creating what, at first glance, might appear to be a plain and practically furnished room.

Christa, who was interested in all aspects of design and fashion, knew better.

But then, no doubt the fees he earned from his spurious 'professional' activities enabled him to enjoy such extravagance.

He had good taste, she had to admit that, Christa acknowledged grimly. The kitchen was actually what she would have chosen for herself had she been able to afford such a luxury. The cupboards might look plain and workmanlike but there was no mistaking the cherrywood's expensive subtle gleam, nor the high quality of the furniture's design.

It would be interesting to see how the rest of the house was furnished.

'Hungry?' she heard Daniel asking her.

'Why?' she asked him. 'Do meals come extra?'

She made no attempt to hide her hostility, but his reaction to it brought a hot, shamed flush to her face as
he told her quietly, 'No, of course they don't. As I've
already said, there'll be no charge for your stay here.
This venture isn't something I've taken on purely to make
money, although I'd be lying if I said that my motives
were completely altruistic. I do have to earn my living,
but profit has never been my sole motivation—for
anything.

'You're determined to think the worst of me, aren't
you?' he accused her almost gently. 'I wonder why.'

Angrily Christa turned her head away from him.

'Stop trying to psychoanalyse me,' she told him irritably. 'And yes, I am hungry...'

'Good, so am I, although I'm afraid it will have to
be something simple: soup and a salad. I'll take you up
to your room first, though. It's this way.'

'This way' turned out to be through a door which led
into a spacious rectangular hallway.

'The house was originally built by the youngest son
of a Victorian industrialist who wanted to return to his
family's roots, hence its size. The fact that very little
land goes with it makes it something of a white elephant
to the local farming community, so I was able to buy it
reasonably cheaply.'

Why was he being so informative? Christa wondered.
As a means of trying to disarm her? Well, it wouldn't
work.

His unsubtle ploys might not impress her, but the
house certainly did, she admitted, as she followed him
upstairs. The Victorian younger son had obviously had
money and a good architect. The house was solidly built,
its style simple and plain.

Christa paused on the stairs to admire the proportions of the dado rail and skirting-board, her eye caught by a newer-looking piece of wood where the rail had obviously been repaired. Unable to resist, she reached out and stroked her fingertips along the wood; the join was so smooth that you couldn't even feel it, and only the slight difference in colour gave the repair away.

'I see you've spotted my repair work. Not many people do.'

Christa turned her head to look in astonishment at Daniel. 'You did this?' she demanded, unable to conceal her surprise.

'Yes, joinery is my hobby... I made the units in the kitchen. My grandfather was a joiner, a true craftsman, justifiably proud of his skill and his work.

'Your room's this way.'

Silently Christa followed him. That easy, friendly manner of his—was it natural or was it merely assumed? Deceit had to be an integral part of his nature, surely, simply by virtue of the way he earned his living? The art of concealment, or of projecting a false image, so polished and perfected that it was easy for him to make others believe the illusions he created.

Look at the way he had deceived her that first afternoon, the way she had been so certain that the warmth, the admiration in the look he was giving her had been real, until his companion had betrayed him.

What would have happened if he hadn't done so, if she had never discovered his real identity, if for instance that afternoon he had been alone, if he had chosen to follow up on the promise of that exchanged look...?

How much damage could he have actually done to her emotions before she had realised the truth?

Her own vulnerability had come as a shock to her. She had thought herself so fireproof to men of his particular type.

There was only one reason that he had brought her here, virtually kidnapping her in order to do so. No man liked being challenged by a woman, especially when that woman won the challenge, and both professionally and financially he could not afford to be defeated.

It was going to be war between them, and he had some pretty devastating weapons in his arsenal, she acknowledged as he stopped outside one of the several doors off the broad corridor.

'I've put you in here,' he told her. 'You've got your own private bathroom.' He pushed open the bedroom door, allowing her to precede him inside it. The room was furnished plainly and simply, with an antique brass bed and a few pieces of highly polished, age-scarred oak furniture, including a desk.

'I'll leave you to settle in and then over supper we can discuss the structure of your course. One of the things we teach here is the importance of harmonious teamwork and its benefits. We find that many executives lose sight of the importance of working alongside others; our culture breeds a need to dominate, a desire for supposed superiority. We aim to redress the effects of that; to teach the benefits of co-existence, of valuing and supporting one another, of integrating with one's colleagues and team-mates.'

'I don't *have* any team-mates,' Christa told him drily. She was on safer ground here, and with every word he spoke she could feel her resistance to what he was saying growing. 'You should try going out into the real world,' she added cynically. 'I promise you, it doesn't work. One of the first things that would happen if I and my fellow importers started empathising supportively with one another is that our buyers would accuse us of setting up a cartel and of price-fixing.'

'You don't fool me, Christa,' Daniel told her softly, by way of response. 'You may think you sound hard and cynical, but that's just a disguise, a form of protection.'

He had gone, closing the door quietly behind him before Christa could summon up a suitable retort.

Her need protection? Ridiculous. Protection from what—from who?

Christa hesitated in the hallway, the temptingly rich smell of soup coaxing her to go into the kitchen, the knowledge that Daniel was waiting inside it for her stopping her. But when the door opened and he appeared in front of her the decision was taken out of her hands.

'Soup's ready,' he told her cheerfully, 'although *I* can't claim much credit. All I had to do was to reheat it in the microwave.'

Who had cooked it? Christa wondered curiously ten minutes later, seated at the kitchen table dipping her spoon into the thick rich broth. A comfortably middle-aged local farmer's wife, or someone else—younger—prettier? Daniel was a very attractive man, both sexually and in other ways, or at least he would have been, she amended hastily, if she didn't have the intelligence to see through that very deceptive maleness and recognise what really lay behind it.

However, not all women were fortunate enough to have the benefit of her past experience and knowledge to protect them.

It would be all too easy, she suspected, fatally easy in fact, for a more vulnerable woman to be taken in by his apparent warmth and caring, his sense of humour and his pseudo-readiness to be open about himself, especially once they had looked into his eyes and seen the look she had thought she had seen when they first met!

Fiercely, she clamped down on the memory of how she had felt then, her body tensing.

'What is it? What's wrong?' Daniel asked her solicitously. 'Soup too hot?'

Thank God he couldn't really read her mind, Christa reflected wryly as she avoided his eyes, shaking her head as she responded guardedly, 'No, it's fine. Very good, in fact. Who made it?'

'I'm not really sure. Some of the local farmers' wives are involved in their own small business, cooking and supplying home-made food,' he explained. 'They cater for functions, speciality events, weddings and the like, and run a stall on market day, and they also provide me with a rota of cooks and staff for the centre when it's in operation.

'This soup was part of a batch of food that was in the centre's freezer. I brought it up here to save it being wasted. Normally I cook for myself or eat at the centre.

'I've drawn up a basic programme outline for your course,' he continued. 'We normally follow a more specialised routine, but in your case...'

'In my case, what?' Christa pounced suspiciously as he opened the folder he was holding. 'What makes my case different? Or can I guess?' she challenged him cynically. 'You've already altered the odds in your own favour by doubling the length of the course, but I can tell you now, it doesn't matter what you say or do, I shan't change my mind,' she told him triumphantly.

Just for a second, the grey eyes hardened slightly as he focused on her. 'The extended length of your course has nothing whatsoever to do with my trying to shorten the odds in my favour, as you put it,' he told her curtly. 'It's simply that without any shared group interaction it will take longer to...'

'To brainwash me,' Christa supplied acidly. 'Why don't you just lock me in my room and starve me into submission?'

He was angry now, Christa recognised, a small thrill of apprehension running down her spine as she saw the way his eyes had darkened, his mouth hardening as he looked at her.

'Don't tempt me,' he told her softly. But then his expression lightened, a brief smile touching his mouth as he said, 'You, submissive...? Somehow I doubt it.'

There was something in the way he was looking at her... something in his smile... Thoroughly flustered, Christa dropped her head.

Damn the man! How had he managed to turn her angry challenge around so that suddenly it was filled with such subtle sexual innuendo that she could actually feel her body starting to grow hot?

'So what exactly *are* you planning to do with me?' she demanded quickly—too quickly, she realised, biting her lip in chagrin as she waited for him to use the verbal slip she had just made; but to her relief, and to her surprise as well, he didn't do so, merely looking down at his file and telling her,

'The course comprises a mixture of physical and mental exercises designed to promote trust in others and to foster an ability to share control through group activities and group discussions.

'The group activities make use of our surroundings and include mountain-walking, where the walkers are paired together, and, similarly, canoeing...'

'Canoeing...' Christa stared at him. 'No way, you can forget that,' she told him, visions of the flimsy, frail craft he was talking about filling her horrified imagination. She could swim—just—preferably in a heated pool with no current and no waves, but if he expected her voluntarily to risk her life...

'There's nothing to be afraid of...' she heard him telling her, as though he had read her mind. 'The canoes are unsinkable; the worst that can happen is that they might roll over if badly handled, but you'll be wearing a wetsuit and...'

'No. No way,' Christa reiterated with angry vehemence.

'I promise you, there really is nothing to fear,' Daniel repeated. 'I am a fully qualified instructor and...'

'I don't damn well care *how* qualified you are,' Christa told him fiercely. 'I am *not* going canoeing.'

'It's an important part of the course; without it... However, if you've changed your mind and you no longer want to go through with the course...'

Wild-eyed with fury, Christa glared at him. She didn't trust herself to speak. If she did... He was trying to trick her, to trap her into giving up, backing down and letting him win by default.

'I hope for your sake you're well insured,' she told him through gritted teeth.

'Very,' he confirmed. 'But, if it's any comfort to you, we haven't drowned a pupil yet.'

'One bruise...just one bruise...' Christa threatened him, ignoring the laughter she could see gleaming in his eyes.

'If canoeing is really a problem for you...' she heard Daniel saying, the laughter gone, his voice once again holding that deep male note of concern which made her feel as though somehow her heart had a huge bruise against it.

'You're my problem,' she told him bitterly. 'You and this whole money-making charade you're running here.'

'Charade!' Now he was angry, Christa recognised, willing herself not to cringe back into her chair as he got up and came towards her, his expression mirroring the anger she could see in his eyes. 'This is no charade. On the contrary, it's something I take extremely seriously.'

'Seriously?' Christa interrupted him scathingly. 'You call sitting round in a circle empathising with one another serious ... climbing mountains and paddling canoes ... ? Oh, and by the way, when exactly does it take place, this trial by water?'

'Most people find it a rather enjoyable experience; however, if you really are afraid, we could ...'

'I am *not* afraid,' Christa denied through gritted teeth. 'I simply don't see the point.'

'You're lying, Christa, you are afraid,' Daniel told her quietly.

'Not of the canoeing,' she shot back fiercely.

'No. Then, what? I wonder. Being proved wrong, perhaps?'

He *was* angry, Christa recognised, despite that quiet voice and his apparent calm.

'No,' she told him spiritedly, 'because I shan't *be* proved wrong. There's no way you can make me change my mind about what you claim you're achieving here.' Or about you, she could have added, but the words stuck in her throat, the triumph of having goaded him into anger for some reason tasting sour on her tongue instead of sweet.

'This whole thing...these...these discussions... these walks, this canoeing,' she told him fiercely. 'They're all just a waste of time...'

'No,' he corrected her, walking away from her to stand by the chair he had just vacated. 'They're not. They are, in fact, an excellent way of fostering trust and mutual reliance.'

'Fostering.' Christa stopped him, her eyebrows rising tauntingly. 'Trust is something that either exists between people or doesn't.'

'Yes, I agree, but sometimes for one reason or another we lose, or even deliberately block out, our ability to trust others, and when that happens it needs to be encouraged to grow and thrive, to be fostered...'

'Or forced?' Christa suggested mock-sweetly, adding with a small shrug, 'Anyway, since I'm here on my own, there doesn't seem to be any point in focusing on that particular aspect of your course, does there? There isn't anyone here for me to learn to trust...'

'Yes, there is,' Daniel told her. 'There's me...'

'You?' Abruptly Christa pushed her soup bowl away. 'You expect me to learn to trust you? Never... That would take a miracle...'

'They have been known to happen,' he reminded her mildly, after a small silence.

'Not this time,' Christa assured him vehemently. 'Wait and see!'

'Besides, learning to trust and to be trusted is an integral part of our course. To know that we can put trust in others and to know that they feel they can trust us increases people's self-esteem—and in a far more positive and valuable way than the often very lonely self-esteem that comes from professional or financial success.

'It's good to know that our work is valued and well rewarded, but it's even better to know that we ourselves are valued for ourselves.'

Christa listened to his speech with wary cynicism. He was good, she had to give him that; that earnest expression, the way he sat slightly forward towards her, the enthusiasm and conviction in his voice. Oh, yes, he was very good, and she could well understand the appeal such a speech would have to battle-scarred careerists.

'I'm sorry, I'm getting carried away with my own enthusiasm,' he apologised, giving her a rueful smile. 'That's the worst of being a convert to your own beliefs.'

'It sounds almost idyllic,' Christa told him coolly. 'But man cannot live by self-esteem alone.'

'Maybe not, but he certainly can't live without it,' Daniel shot back. 'That's been proved over and over again by any number of studies. Take away a human being's self-esteem and you turn life into what is merely existence.'

'You make it sound as though boosting people's self-esteem is some kind of instant "cure-all" for all their ills,' Christa told him.

She made her comment mockingly sarcastic, but to her surprise, instead of retaliating to her taunt, Daniel merely said quietly, 'In many ways I believe it is.

'When I was fifteen my father was made redundant; three months later he killed himself. He was forty-three and he couldn't bear the shame of losing his job. The fact that we loved him, that he was a valued and valuable part of our local community, the fact that we needed him, simply wasn't enough.'

Christa swallowed hard in shocked silence. His simple words, devoid of rhetoric and theatrical fervour, had touched her deeply.

Perhaps because of the loss of her own parents, she was sharply aware of all that he was not saying.

Tears blurred her eyes; she wanted to reach out and touch him, to tell him that she understood.

'Perhaps because of his death financial and professional success have never held much appeal for me. And the thing was that after his death we discovered some shares he had bought several years earlier. He had always enjoyed ''gambling'' in a very small way on the stock market. A takeover resulted in those shares increasing dramatically in value.

'So dramatically, in fact, that my father would never have needed to worry about money again.

'The money I used to buy this estate came from those shares. It seemed a fitting way to use it.'

Christa swallowed again. He seemed so genuine, so...everything she had always wanted a man...*her* man to be.

And yet, at the same time, he was engaged in a business which she knew from experience attracted men who were adept at deceit, men who were little more than an up-market, polished version of confidence tricksters.

Her instincts, her femininity, wanted her to reach out towards him, to believe in him, but her knowledge, her experience, warned her not to do so.

Which one of them was right?

Why not keep an open mind? her heart whispered recklessly. Why not allow him to prove himself to you one way or the other? After all, isn't that what you're here for? Isn't it only fair to have an open mind, to suspend your prejudice against his type? To... to what? To allow herself to fall in love with him and risk being hurt... destroyed as her friend had been?

No. No... there was no way she was going to fall into that trap, however plausible, however genuine, however desirable he might seem.

No way at all.

CHAPTER FOUR

CHRISTA struggled sleepily to sit up in bed. What time was it? Her eyes widened slightly as she looked at her watch. She couldn't remember the last time she had slept so deeply—or for so long. A circumstance which, no doubt, Daniel would state was one of the recuperative effects he claimed for his remote habitat.

Christa had other ideas and she wondered, a little darkly, just what exactly had been in that bedtime mug of cocoa he had insisted on making for her. Cocoa! She had stopped drinking *that* when she left home to go to university.

The house felt quiet and still...and empty...

Frowning, she swung her feet out of bed, reaching for her robe. Last night, Daniel had said that they would spend the morning going over the details of her course.

'Obviously it will vary in some ways from those we normally run.'

'Obviously,' Christa had agreed drily. 'After all, the people you usually deal with are already converts, aren't they?'

'Not exactly,' Daniel had contradicted her, adding firmly, 'And besides, they aren't *here* to be converted but to be *helped* to recognise the signs of stress and to learn how to deal with them and how to integrate well with the rest of the human race and their colleagues in particular.'

'Have you ever thought of taking up the diplomatic services as a career?' Christa had muttered sardonically under her breath, but not quietly enough, it seemed, because he had given her a disconcertingly level look and told her,

'Not really; I don't have the patience for it, or the subtlety.'

Christa had been tempted to argue with him, but was deterred by the huge yawn that had unexpectedly and embarrassingly overtaken her.

'You're tired,' Daniel had commented, getting up from his chair, adding wryly, 'Or perhaps I'm boring you.'

Did he really intend her to answer that question? Christa wondered grimly. He must surely already know that 'boring' was the last thing that any sane member of her sex was likely to find him.

Where was he now? Somehow, without knowing *how* she knew it, she sensed that he wasn't in the house.

She padded over to the window, pulling back the curtains and blinking in the unexpected shock of the brightness of the morning light. The sky was a sharp, clear blue, the sunlight pale and very bright.

As she blinked in its glare she wasn't sure, at first, if the white dazzle she could see capping the range of mountains that surrounded them was caused by the sunlight or if in fact it was actually snow.

She blinked again, clearing her vision, her jaw dropping slightly as she recognised that it was indeed snow. Uncomfortably she remembered her scornful words to Daniel the previous day.

Snow in October?

'Wales is another country,' he had warned her, and now, abruptly, this mountainous, semi-barren region did seem very alien and even slightly intimidating. She had heard on the news, had read of climbers being lost in snowdrifts and blizzards in the Scottish and Welsh mountains at times of the year when the mere idea of snow in other parts of the country seemed laughable.

In a city environment, in the more heavily populated areas of the country, it was easy to forget that these mountains existed.

'I promise you that by the time you leave here you will see yourself and everyone, *everything* around you, in a different light,' Daniel had promised her, quietly, last night.

'How?' she had challenged him scathingly.

'Wait and see,' he had told her.

She shivered slightly, as though she could actually feel the icy chill of those snow-clad peaks, even though she was actually standing in the centrally heated protection of a warm bedroom.

Was it possible that the process of change had begun already in her reaction to the sight of the mountains, her awareness of her own unexpected awe of them . . . ?

Don't be ridiculous, she chided herself fiercely. All right, so it *had* been a shock to see those snow-covered peaks, but what a ridiculous idea to feel that her position had somehow been undermined, her stance threatened.

Daniel was hardly personally responsible for the snow, was he?

When she left Wales, it wouldn't be with her views changed, but rather with them reinforced. When she returned home it would be to confirm what she already believed. Daniel might appear genuine and sincere in his beliefs, he might even actually believe in them himself, but he wouldn't be able to convince her. While his 'converts' faithfully played out the roles he had taught them, others, shrewder, less easily persuadable, would take advantage of them to advance their own interests; that was a fact of human nature.

But if Daniel *was* right, if people *could* learn to focus themselves, to draw their sense of self-worth from a far less materialistic and competitive source, then . . .

Impossible, she told herself quickly—other than in an ideal world peopled by ideal human beings.

She tensed as a sound outside caught her attention, frowning as she strained to listen. It sounded as though someone was working out there. Daniel? Working at *what*? Wasn't *she* supposed to be his work?

If *this* was his way of trying to convert her—simply ignoring her—then . . . Or was *he* perhaps having second thoughts? Perhaps he had begun to recognise that she was no easy pushover . . . Had he even begun to give up?

Quickly selecting clean clothes, she hurried into the bathroom. If she could get him to admit that he had been wrong then she could leave here, go back to her real life, now, before . . .

Before what? Before she started to forget why she was here and began to focus instead, not on reality, but on fantasy, to close her eyes and allow herself to be seduced by her body's female response to Daniel's subtly potent maleness?

Ridiculous! As though she of all people would be stupid enough to do any such thing.

Downstairs the kitchen was empty—and scrupulously neat and tidy; there was a note on the table addressed to her. She read it quickly, trying to quell the sudden quickened pace of her heartbeat as she studied Daniel's firm handwriting.

'Looked in on you at seven, but decided to let you go on sleeping. Help yourself to breakfast.'

He had looked in on her.

Christa swallowed uncomfortably, her body suddenly very hot. It disturbed her to think of him looking at her when she was asleep and oblivious to his presence, vulnerable. Her face grew even hotter as she remembered the way her nightshirt had of coming unfastened and sliding off her shoulder.

He had had no right to come into her bedroom, she decided crossly, and when she saw him she would tell him so.

She made herself some coffee, too on edge to want anything to eat, curiosity drawing her outside once she had finished it to make her way across the yard in the direction of the noise she had heard earlier.

It was colder outside than she had expected; the fine wool of the designer trouser suit she had bought as a piece of shameful self-indulgence wasn't thick enough to protect her legs from the sharp wind, and she regretted leaving the house without her jacket when she felt the gooseflesh lifting her chilled skin beneath the thin cloth on her body.

She was just about to turn round and go back inside for her jacket when a noise behind her stopped her.

Her heart suddenly started to beat faster with nervous apprehension as she recognised the sound of hooves on the cobbles of the farmyard and, sure enough, when she turned round there was Clarence, standing between her and the house, watching her with a malevolent expression.

Christa felt her stomach lurch with fear. As a child she had visited her grandmother who had kept a goat.

Christa had been taken by her mother to see the young kids, all white-haired and silky-soft to touch, but the nanny for some reason had objected to their presence and had charged them.

Neither Christa's mother nor her grandmother had been particularly perturbed, but to Christa it had been a terrifying experience and one she had never totally forgotten.

She had felt a brief resurgence of that fear yesterday, but viewing Clarence from the dual safety of the Land Rover and Daniel's protective bulk was a very different thing from being alone in the farmyard with him, knowing both that he stood between her and safety and that he could outrun her if she gave in to her fear and fled.

It was almost as though he *knew* how she felt, Christa acknowledged nervously, as his attention was momentarily diverted from her trousers.

'One bite out of these and you're dead,' she warned him threateningly, but she could have sworn that he was laughing at her, recognising her complete inability to do anything to protect either her trousers or herself.

He took a step towards her, and then another.

Christa could feel her heart racing, her mouth going dry.

'Shoo,' she told him shakily. 'Shoo...go away...go away...'

Her voice sounded weak and thready, as ineffectual against the animal's malignant supremacy as her words. Was this really her—the same woman who had stood her ground and won the day against the most subtle and skilled bargainers of the Indian subcontinent?

Somewhere on the periphery of her awareness she was vaguely conscious of the fact that the rhythmic tapping

of metal against stone had stopped, but she was too
afraid of the animal in front of her to recognise what
the cessation of noise really meant, so that Daniel's warm
and obviously amused, 'Ah, you're up, good... I was
just thinking it was time I took a break for lunch,' came
as a complete surprise.

At any other time Christa would have responded instantly and angrily to his teasing, pointing out that if he
did indeed have lunch at ten o'clock in the morning he
was a very unusual person, but the shock of hearing his
voice, combined with her fear, caused her instead to spin
round wildly, her fear of the goat momentarily super-
seded by the humiliation of having Daniel witness her
predicament.

Almost as though he had been waiting for it to happen,
for her concentration to waver, their eye-contact broken,
Clarence took advantage of the opportunity she had
given him, charging towards her with Machiavellian glee.

Christa heard the rushing sound of his charge and
swung back round, her defensive awareness of Daniel's
watchful amusement forgotten, drowned by the sheer tide
of shocked fear that overwhelmed her. Her eyes dilating
with terror, she reacted instinctively, turning round to
run, to escape; only her thin city shoes were not designed for muddy cobbles, and the small part of her brain
that could still function rationally was already telling her
that no mere human being on two legs could ever hope
to outrun a gleefully malevolent animal on four.

Her heart pounding with suffocating dread, she was
once again that small girl at her grandmother's, knowing
that there was no escape, that...

Her heart gave one final terrified bound as the ground
suddenly fell away beneath her, only it wasn't the wet
muddy cobbles she found herself lying against, with
Clarence breathing hotly over her prone body, but the

solid, safe, comforting warmth of another human body and a pair of strong protective human—male—arms holding her tight.

Human...male... *Daniel*.

Christa opened the eyes she had squeezed tightly shut in panic.

Daniel! Daniel was holding her. Daniel's arms were wrapped firmly around her body, Daniel's hand sliding into her hair as he gently pressed her face into the warm curve of his throat, *Daniel's* voice, warm and alive, trembling slightly with what might just have been a hint of teasing laughter as he said softly against her ear, 'Hey, come on, it's all right. It's only Clarence, that's all.'

That's all!

Indignantly Christa lifted her head and looked at him. 'He was going to attack me,' she told him shakily, biting down hard on her lip as she remembered how frightened she had been.

Her whole body started to tremble and go weak; she felt cold all over and slightly nauseous, the tears she had held back earlier betrayingly flooding her eyes.

'It's all right for you,' she told Daniel angrily, '*you* think it's funny, but...'

Proudly she struggled to fight free of the arm he still had wrapped around her, even though she was acutely conscious of the fact that Clarence was still here, albeit now keeping a polite and almost benign distance from them.

'No, I don't think it's funny,' Daniel contradicted her. His voice, like the touch of his hand against her face, held something—a quality, an emotion—that made her hold her breath, afraid of either recognising or acknowledging it.

'Let me go,' she demanded, but her voice sounded thready and weak, lacking conviction.

'In a minute, when I've got you safely back inside. There really isn't any need for you to be afraid of Clarence, you know,' Daniel told her as he turned her round and started to guide her back towards the house.

'He attacked me,' Christa told him.

'He's a bully; he could sense your fear and made use of it as all bullies do. But it wasn't just Clarence who frightened you, was it?' he guessed astutely as he opened the back door for her.

'No,' Christa admitted curtly. 'There was... my grandmother had a goat and I was terrified of it. She used to laugh at me, tell me not to be silly, say that life would hold many more things for me to be afraid of than a bad-tempered nanny goat. She despised weakness in people. She was a very strong woman.'

She frowned as she saw the way Daniel was looking at her.

'What is it?' she asked him uncertainly. 'Why are you looking at me like that?'

'I was just thinking about the child you must have been...'

'Well, don't,' Christa cautioned him sharply. 'I'm not a child any more, I'm a woman, and——'

'I know...'

Something in the soft, subtle undertone to the words made her look at him, her whole body suddenly enveloped in a sharp sense of awareness, of knowing.

'Very, very much a woman,' Daniel told her quietly.

'No.'

Her denial was automatic, but so weakly ineffectual that Christa wasn't at all surprised when he ignored it, reaching out to take hold of her, his hands spanning her waist and then moving caressingly up over her back and then down again to her hips, a look of such intense sensual pleasure in his eyes that it shocked her into immobility.

If any other man had experienced such intense pleasure just touching her he had certainly never let her know it, never let her see how much the shape of her body, the warmth of her skin beneath his fingertips pleased him.

She knew that Daniel was going to kiss her, knew it and did nothing at all to stop him, and nothing at all either to control the tiny quiver that ran betrayingly through her body.

All her senses focused on what she knew was going to happen, on the slow, long-drawn-out build of anticipation, the careful touch of Daniel's hands as he cupped her face, his fingertips tracing its shape, leaving hot trails of fire against her skin; she could see the sharp lift of his chest as though he was having trouble drawing the air to breathe, see the intense concentration in his eyes as they darkened with desire. Desire for her.

Her heart jerked dangerously against her ribs, her own breath unsteady and erratic; his mouth touched her skin, his fingers pushing her hair back from her face, stroking the soft skin just behind her ear, making her tremble and close her eyes, the small sound that could have either been denial or pleasure muted in her throat as his lips followed the path of his fingertips.

She could feel her whole body starting to shiver with delight, to come alive, and without making any conscious effort to move she was suddenly standing closer to Daniel, so close that she could actually feel the heavy, unsteady thud of his heartbeat, the tension in his muscles, the warmth of his flesh beneath hands she hadn't even realised she had raised to touch him.

Dizzily she watched the strong pulse thudding at the base of his throat, felt the heat coming off his body, the subtle change from controlled exploration to less controllable desire in the movement of his lips against her skin—and her own response to it.

She wanted him. Against all logic, all reason, she was conscious of a chemistry between them, a desire for him that was so strong that, even though it ran completely contrary to what she wanted to feel, she was totally powerless to control it.

A feeling of fear and panic filled her but instead of strengthening her need to pull away from him, to stop what was happening, all it did was increase her weakness, her inability to resist the powerful flood engulfing her.

She *did* try to stop him, to protest, but her shakily whispered words were lost, silenced by the warm pressure of his mouth as he gathered her closely, kissing her with such soft, slow determination that it felt as though her whole body was dissolving and melting into him, and not merely her willpower.

No man had ever kissed her like this before, made her feel like this, not just aroused to physical desire, but filled with so much emotion that it made her eyes burn with tears behind her closed eyelids and her throat ache with yearning, every bit as much as her body ached with longing.

She had no will, no life, no power that was not controlled by him, her mind, her body, her emotions joyously obedient to the increasing demand of his mouth, the subtle caress of his tongue as it stroked persuasively against her lips coaxing them to soften and to part, to allow him the kind of intimacy she had somehow always believed she was too fastidious ever to want to enjoy.

Enjoy... No way did that small, simple word encompass the sensations, the emotions that poured through her now, sensitising every inch of her body, both outside and in, to such an extent that she could scarcely bear the heavy pressure of her clothes against her skin, nor control her shuddering reaction to the caress of Daniel's hands, the hot hard pressure of his body.

'No...' Frantically Christa pushed herself away from Daniel, breaking their kiss, and the dark, magnetic sorcery of her unwanted and far too dangerous thoughts.

Her face burned hotly with chagrin. She could scarcely recognise herself in the wanton eroticism of her thoughts and desires.

When Daniel moved towards her as though he intended to take her back in his arms, for a shocked heartbeat of time Christa actually felt that she wanted him to, that she actually wanted him to take hold of her and silence her protests with the hard, passionate demand of his mouth, to physically overrule the logic of her thoughts and allow her body, her senses, the aching desire and need that crawled so treacherously through the pit of her stomach to her head.

Her heart jerked violently against her ribs in a mixture of fear and shock, the panic of knowing how close she had come to totally losing all self-control propelling her into another step back.

She saw Daniel frown, the hand he had stretched out towards her dropping to his side, the smile slowly dying from his eyes.

'I'm going back inside,' Christa told him shortly.

No wonder he had stopped smiling at her. Sickly she wondered how many other women before her had been deceived by the false promise of his oh, so seductive kiss, the sensual delicacy of his touch, the pseudo-vulnerable tension in his body as he released her, as though he could hardly bear to let her go, the quick way in which he had turned his body slightly away from her as though trying to disguise its erotic arousal.

Oh, he knew all the tricks, how it made a woman feel to know that she excited him so much and to know that he wanted to protect her from his arousal.

The hot tears stinging her eyes as she hurried, head down, across the kitchen, and the faint tremor in her body, weren't just caused by the fright Clarence had given her. Tellingly, as she reached the door, against all her own better judgement she stopped to turn her head to look at Daniel.

He was standing motionless, watching her, his hands on his hips, his forearms bare, his hair, like the soft cotton open neck of his shirt, ruffled slightly by the breeze through the open back door.

Could he see from that distance the soft flush that was engulfing her body; did he *know* that *he* was the cause of it; did he *care* about what he was doing to her, about the pain he could potentially cause her?

No, of course he didn't. His kind of man never did, Christa reflected bitterly, as she turned on her heel—and her hand pushed open the hall door.

Her shoes, she noticed, the expensive, soft leather loafers she had bought herself as a special treat only months ago, were thick with mud; there were splashes of it on her trousers, and the breeze, which had done little more than flauntingly caress Daniel's skin, highlighting the strong play of muscles beneath the tanned flesh of his arms, had much more unkindly reduced her flesh to pinched, goose-fleshed chilliness.

It was too late now to regret not packing the thermal underwear which had served her so well all through last winter, she admitted morosely as she went back upstairs in search of something warm to put on.

But once she reached her bedroom, instead of completing the task which had brought her there, she went instead to stand unseeingly in front of her bedroom window, oblivious to the magnificence of the view beyond it, the mountains, stark and awesome, their sheer sides falling away from the snow-capped pinnacles. Her thoughts instead were locked on those few minutes she had spent in Daniel's arms.

A small, sharply self-judgemental sound of anger escaped from her lips.

How could it have happened? How could she have allowed it to happen . . . wanted it to happen?

'No.' The husky denial came too late to stop the insidious, mocking question her subconscious slid so damningly into her mind. She had not wanted it to happen; she had not . . .

Not what? Not wanted Daniel to kiss her?

Her body trembled. She closed her eyes against the self-torment of the inner taunt, knowing full well that she could not rebuff the mocking whispered question without lying.

She had wanted Daniel to kiss her, to touch her, to . . .

This was crazy; she was an adult, for heaven's sake, far too mature, too sensible, too aware to fall head over heels in love with a man simply because his kisses did things to her that no man had ever come anywhere near doing before.

Head over heels in love. That spinning, dizzying, frighteningly disorientating feeling, as though the ground was no longer completely stable under her feet, could not have been caused, surely, by something as simple as the threat of having fallen in love with Daniel?

A threat which was surely laughable in its complete impossibility.

Yes, she might be sexually attracted to him, she admitted cautiously, and yes, it had been a mistake—and one which she would not repeat—to allow that attraction to get the upper hand and make her behave with unfamiliar recklessness; but in love... No... Never. Not her, and certainly not with a man like Daniel.

If she was to stay here...

If. There was no 'if' about it. She had to stay, she reminded herself sharply. If she left now, not just Daniel but everyone at home would assume that it was because she could no longer stand by her outspoken statements.

She had to stay, and she had to find a way of controlling her unwanted sexual awareness of him. Remember what had happened to Laura. Laura had fallen in love too, and look what had happened to her.

Character-building mountain hikes, team-building exercises, *canoeing*!

Angrily Christa threw down the programmes Daniel had given her. Did he really think any of that was going to change her mind?

The canoeing trip was fixed for tomorrow. She frowned as she looked out of the window. She could just see the silver gleam of water where the lake reflected the cold grey-blue of the sky.

She had never really been an outdoors type; she liked the heat and the sunshine, not the cold and the wet; her most recent experience of being afloat had been in the Greek islands, a far cry from Wales, and the captain of the Greek craft had been nothing like Daniel—nothing at all, she reflected, mentally contrasting the Greek's portly, sturdy body with Daniel's: the cold grey dullness of the Welsh mountains now that the early morning brightness had gone with the warmth and sunshine of the Aegean sea; and, before she could stop herself, Daniel's normal apparel of jeans and shirt with a pair of faded cut-off shorts, the rest of his body bare beneath the hot Greek sun apart from the fine, soft covering of dark hair that ran so tantalisingly from his breastbone to the waistband of his shorts.

Her mouth, Christa discovered, as she fiercely dismissed the tantalising mental image her traitorous senses had called up, had gone very dry and her pulse was very fast.

Well, at least she needn't worry about Daniel wearing nothing more than a pair of shorts tomorrow, she acknowledged wryly. Wetsuits were apparently to be the order of the day.

It infuriated her that she should be so perversely and so ridiculously affected by Daniel as a man.

It wasn't *just* angry impatience with herself that she felt, though, was it? There were other emotions there as well. Anxiety, apprehension...uncertainty and...

Tiredly she closed her eyes. It wasn't *logical* that she should feel desire for such a man; that she should want him...ache for him. Such feelings would have to be suppressed...destroyed...denied.

'Ready.'

Christa threw Daniel a murderous look as he stood at the side of the small jetty waiting for her. They had changed into their wetsuits in the changing-room provided inside the small but well-equipped boat-house next to the jetty, and now Daniel was standing next to the wooden ladder leading down to the water.

Gritting her teeth, Christa walked towards him. Below her on the water she could see the canoe, an impossibly fragile thing, bouncing lightly on the waves.

'You can't possibly expect me to risk my life in *that*,' she protested in disbelief. It looked like a child's toy.

'It's perfectly safe,' Daniel assured her. 'Completely unsinkable; the worst you can do is turn turtle in it...'

'Turn turtle?' Christa demanded suspiciously.

'Yes,' he agreed, explaining, 'An inexperienced canoeist can cause it to capsize, but these things are specially designed so that they right themselves again without any damage to either themselves or the people in them. That's why we use them.

'You'll be perfectly safe, Christa. I wouldn't take you out in it if you weren't...'

'Oh, no?' Christa muttered under her breath, but he had obviously heard her, because she just caught the hard gleam of anger in his eyes before he masked it and asked her lightly,

'What were you expecting: that I'd take you out to the middle of the lake and threaten you with death by drowning if you didn't agree to change your mind?'

She hadn't thought anything of the kind, of course, but now, hearing him say the words and seeing the open amusement in his eyes made her feel so defensive and angry that she retaliated acidly, 'I wouldn't put it past you. After all, you must be pretty desperate. A place like this succeeds or fails on its reputation...'

'And you have sufficient influence to ensure that success or failure?' Daniel asked her silkily.

It was a justifiable taunt, Christa knew, but even so it still surprised her. *She* was the one who made the nasty snide comments, not Daniel.

'Oh, for heaven's sake, let's just get the whole thing over and done with,' she demanded sourly.

It was a cold, grey day, the sky threatening rain, the wind whipping the surface of the lake into angry, choppy little waves.

Christa shivered as she looked at them and then looked back at the brightly painted canoe. But she wasn't going to reveal her apprehension, to back down and have Daniel taunt her.

Taking a deep breath, she walked to the end of the jetty.

'I'll go down first,' Daniel told her.

There was nothing uncertain or lacking in confidence about the way *he* headed down the wooden ladder and eased himself easily into one of the canoe's two small spaces, Christa acknowledged grudgingly, watching as he manoeuvred the small craft close to the bottom of the ladder and then told her to come down.

Far less confidently Christa did so, shivering a little as she reached the last rung of the ladder.

'It's all right, you're doing fine,' she heard Daniel telling her. 'Now, just step over here and ease yourself into the canoe.'

For a moment she was tempted to refuse. Her mouth had gone uncomfortably dry, her body tensing as she clung to the ladder. Daniel was holding the canoe stable, one hand on the ladder, the other reaching out to help her, but if he let go...

'It's all right, Christa...'

Chagrined that he had so easily seen her fear, Christa gritted her teeth and stepped forward.

She had a wild moment of panic as she let go of the ladder and eased herself down into the canoe, but she fought it down, willing herself not to betray her feelings

in front of Daniel, and then blessedly she was neatly
tucked inside the small craft and Daniel was reaching
for the paddle, sending them skimming across the grey
surface of the lake at a speed that made Christa catch
her breath. Even through the thickness of his wetsuit he
could see the powerful strength of his shoulder muscles.

No need to wonder now, with that perverse feminine
curiosity, where a man who was primarily an academic
had come by them.

'Normally in this exercise we send a group of four
students out with one instructor in one of our larger
canoes, initially.

'Once he has demonstrated all the safety techniques
and he is satisfied that they know the basics of handling
the craft, he then removes all but two of the paddles,
which are given to separate members of the group. They,
then, between them, have to make their way back to the
jetty by co-ordinating their paddling and directions in a
group effort where they are all mutually dependent on
one another.'

'Sounds like a recipe for mass murder,' Christa told
him sardonically. 'If something like that happened in
real life, one of them would try to gain control of both
paddles and then...'

'And then what? They wouldn't be able to keep control
of them and manoeuvre the craft while holding the others
at bay, would they?' Daniel reasoned.

'They could dispose of the others, kill them with the
paddle, push them overboard...'

'Mmm...they *could*, but wouldn't it make much more
sense for them to work together, to share the task of
reaching dry land?'

'In a perfect world, perhaps, but this isn't a perfect
world,' Christa pointed out irritably.

'No. Then maybe we should try harder to make it one...'

He couldn't really think she was gullible enough to believe he actually thought such idealism could work—could he? Christa wondered derisively.

They were well out into the middle of the lake now and the small waves had become much higher and stronger.

'What would you do now, Christa, if we were to lose both our paddles?'

'Sue?' Christa suggested sweetly.

Daniel laughed.

'You'd have to get back to dry land first,' he pointed out to her.

'I can swim,' Christa told him.

'It's a long way and the water's very cold. Try thinking a little more laterally,' he coaxed her. 'Hands can make very good paddles, especially with the two of us working together, but first one of us would have to get up and turn round.'

'There's no way I'd turn my back on you...' Christa answered immediately. 'No way!'

'So you'd prefer to stay out here rather than risk giving me your trust? Fine,' Daniel told her calmly, but there was a glint in his eyes that warned her he was losing patience with her, and then, to her horror, he let go of the paddles, and while Christa was staring at them in disbelief, watching them float away, he stood up in one easy motion and lowered himself into the water.

'Daniel, what are you doing? You *can't leave* me here like this,' Christa protested in panic as he released the canoe and started to swim towards the shore.

He paused, treading water as he turned to look at her.

'It was your choice, Christa,' he told her.

Her choice. *Her* choice to be abandoned here in the middle of a lake that was God alone knew how deep and filled with icy cold water.

Daniel was several yards away now and quite obviously had no intention of turning back.

Panic filled her, but her pride wouldn't let her call out to him. One of the paddles was still floating tantalisingly close by. Using her hands, she steered towards it and then reached out to grab hold of it, only she wasn't quite close enough and she had reached over too far.

The feeling that hit her as she felt the canoe capsize and the cold lake-water drench her made the panic Clarence had induced in her fade to a mere nothing.

She did everything she knew logically she ought not to do, from crying out and gulping in mouthfuls of water to thrashing around in the lake instead of keeping still, convinced that her last moment had come and that she was about to drown.

The realisation that the canoe had righted itself; that she was no longer lying in the water and that, moreover, Daniel had turned back and was deftly manoeuvring himself back into the craft in front of her, instead of bringing her relief caused her to feel an intense and overwhelming surge of furious anger spiked with chagrin. So intense, in fact, that her whole body trembled under the grip of it as it rendered her totally speechless.

But not for long.

The moment Daniel brought the canoe alongside the jetty she scrambled up the ladder, waiting for him to join her, her stance as militant as the glitter in her eyes as she accused.

'You did that deliberately, didn't you? You tried to drown me...' she accused furiously.

'No, Christa... You panicked and capsized the canoe, but I promise you, you were never in any danger of drowning...'

'So you say... Just what the hell were you trying to do?'

'I was trying to show you the benefits of allowing yourself to trust.'

'And punishing me when I refused to do so by half terrifying me to death...'

'*You* were the one who punished *yourself*. There wasn't anything for you to fear.'

'I've only got your word for that—oh, I can see what you're up to,' Christa told him, refusing to listen. 'If you can't get people to agree with you voluntarily, you force them into it by terrifying them. Well, it won't work with me, Daniel. In my view you're nothing but an arrogant, irresponsible...'

To her consternation she couldn't go on. Her teeth had started to chatter and, even more ominously, her legs had gone so weak that the only thing keeping her upright was her willpower.

From a distance she could hear Daniel telling her curtly, 'Has it occurred to you that those same adjectives could quite easily be used to describe you, Christa? Christa!'

She could hear the way his voice changed, concern replacing contempt, but the sound seemed to reach her from a long way away, and the feeling of being scooped up in his arms, instead of arousing fresh anger, rather oddly filled her with a delicious sense of warmth and comfort.

Her dunking in the lake had obviously affected her far more than she had realised, she acknowledged five minutes later, as she stood unprotesting and unfam-

iliarly docile beneath the blessedly warm spray of one
of the boat-house showers, while Daniel stood there with
her, quickly peeling off her wetsuit.

'It's all right, Christa, you're going to be fine. You're
in shock that's all,' she heard him telling her as he turned
off the warm water and wrapped her in a big towel. But
it had been *his* eyes that had darkened before he'd looked
firmly away from her naked body, his hands that had
trembled briefly when he had touched her.

And, beneath the shock that was still making her teeth
chatter and her body tremble, Christa was aware of a
small surge of feminine triumph in the knowledge that
the sight of her naked body had affected him—so much
so that, as a man, he had been almost afraid to look at
her or touch her, that she was not the only one to feel
unawakened desire, even if he'd very quickly cloaked his
desire in clinical detachment.

Just as soon as he had assured himself that she was
not in any real danger from her shock, he had left her
to dress herself while he too got changed. But if, instead
of going, he had looked at her a second time, touched
her... It had shocked her to feel that very betraying shock
of sensation that ran through her body, especially when,
mentally and emotionally, she was still so furiously angry
with him.

Half an hour later, as she sat beside him while he drove
the Land Rover back to the farm, she was still just as
angry—with herself as well as with him. *Why* had she
panicked like that, giving him the opportunity to... to
what? To make her feel even more wary of the physical
effect he had on her?

'How are you feeling now?'

'Fine—no thanks to you,' she told him pithily, adding furiously as her anger overwhelmed her, 'God knows what you were trying to prove, but...'

'I wasn't trying to *prove* anything,' he cut in tersely.

Christa could see the anger in his eyes as well as hear it in his voice, but instead of feeling pleased that she had breached his professional detachment there was an oddly painful lump in her throat.

'I don't think I've ever met anyone so stubbornly determined to hang on to their prejudices as you, Christa. What is it that you're really afraid of?'

'The fact that you can't make me change my mind or my opinions doesn't mean I'm afraid. Far from it,' Christa told him fiercely, but she knew that she wasn't being entirely honest, and she couldn't sustain the long, level eye-contact he was making with her.

As she turned her head away from him she could feel her colour starting to rise slightly.

'What were you expecting, anyway?' she demanded aggressively, to cover her vulnerability. 'That that little sermon you delivered out there on the lake would make me fling myself into your arms and declare my undying trust in you?'

Even as she spoke she knew she had gone too far, betrayed far more than was wise with that foolish comment about flinging herself into his arms, taken the situation into intensely personal realms which Daniel, as a professional, couldn't fail to interpret correctly, despite the scorn she had injected into her voice.

'Nothing quite so theatrical,' she heard him telling her grittily. 'A simple open-minded willingness to listen without pre-judging, that was all I wanted from you, Christa, but of course I might just as well have asked for the moon, mightn't I?' he concluded bitterly, braking with such force as he swung the Land Rover round a tight bend that Christa was thrown heavily against him.

The scent of his skin, clean and faintly soapy, made her stomach lurch with such intensity that she had to dig her nails into the palms of her hands to prevent herself from crying out in shock.

How *could* she be so physically and sensuously responsive to him?

It was a question that continued to torment her for the rest of the day, and her secret, silent worrying at it caused Daniel to frown as he watched her.

Her dunking in the lake had not been planned, but theoretically, once over the initial shock of it, she was physically and mentally strong enough to throw off the effects very quickly, her recovery aided by the intensity of her fury against him. But, instead of verbally castigating him now, as he had expected, she had become very quiet and withdrawn.

'Christa... Are you sure you're feeling OK...?'

'What's wrong?' she asked him sourly. 'Afraid that I might die of pneumonia or something?'

Her speedy verbal retaliation reassured him, causing his eyes to gleam slightly with amusement as he told her dulcetly, 'I know how determined you are to discredit the work I'm doing here, but somehow I doubt that even you would want to go to quite those lengths...'

'Don't bet on it,' Christa told him childishly, darkly. 'It might almost be worth it.'

'What is it—what's wrong?'

Christa tensed as Daniel broke off in the middle of explaining his theories and teaching methods to her to pose the concerned question.

They were in his study, a warm, cheerful room decorated in rich terracottas and soft greens; bookshelves crammed with books covering a fascinatingly wide range of subjects filled the walls; a fire burned warmly in the grate, and everything about the room and its décor encouraged relaxation. But relaxing was the last thing Christa felt able to do. Not when Daniel had just returned from feeding the fire not to his chair but to her side, as she sat at the desk, studying the papers he had given her.

Now as he leaned over her, one hand on the back of her chair, the other on the desk only inches away from her own, she was conscious of the heat rising up through her body, and with it the panic that sent her heartbeat into overdrive and made the blood roar dizzily in her ears.

She was so acutely conscious of him that she could actually smell him—not the faint sharp tang of the cold mountain air he had brought in with him when he went out for some logs, but *him*.

The knowledge that she was conscious of him so intimately made the flush burning her skin deepen and her body start to tremble.

Not even then was the runaway panic of her denial strong enough to suppress the jumble of rapid-fire mental images flashing across her brain: Daniel holding her in his arms, Daniel, his body naked as he touched her and caressed her. Daniel filmed slightly with sweat, the totally male scent of his desire and arousal flooding her responsive senses with messages her body ached to reciprocate.

'Christa, what is it? Your face is burning up ...'

Christa wasn't sure which of them was the more shocked at the way she cried out and visibly cringed away from his touch as he reached out to touch her skin.

'I'm all right... It's nothing. It's just hot in here,' she fibbed. 'I...I was standing by the fire while you were out,' she added equally untruthfully, holding her breath nervously in case he challenged her lie, but fortunately he seemed to accept it, although he was still frowning.

'For a woman who has made her views on what we're trying to do here extremely plain, so far you've been surprisingly unargumentative,' he told her wryly.

'Not because I've changed my mind,' Christa assured him; she was on safer ground here...much safer. 'In theory what you're saying sounds good,' she acknowledged, adding with a slightly cynical twist to her lips, 'Very high-minded and altruistic.'

'But you don't accept that they are,' Daniel replied for her.

He was watching her intently—too intently, Christa acknowledged. She waited for her answer, but there was no sign that anything she had said had disturbed him, she admitted—far from it.

'Why?' he challenged her.

'Why?' Christa repeated almost stupidly, her thoughts wandering from the subject under discussion to her own vulnerability towards him and the problems it was causing her. Not the least of which was the funny ache in the region of her heart and the awful compulsion to reach out and touch him which seemed to have gripped her.

Was it possible for something to happen to a person so that their behaviour and emotions were completely the opposite of what they wanted them to be?

Yes, and it was called insanity, she told herself starkly, hastily collecting her thoughts as she realised that Daniel was still waiting for her response.

'Yes, why don't you accept that my motives are altruistic?'

'Well, there are the fees you charge to attend your courses for a start,' Christa told him drily. 'They are hardly altruistic, are they?'

'Perhaps not, but they are a fair reflection of what it costs to run a venture like this, to provide the highly skilled and professional tuition that is necessary.'

'And to enable you to make a handsome profit into the bargain,' Christa suggested.

Now she felt that she had really angered him.

'Is that really what you think of me?' he asked her quietly, cutting right across the defences she had erected and bringing the question at issue out of the public arena into one that was strictly private with such speed that she felt as though the ground had been cut completely from beneath her feet.

'This has nothing to do with what I think of you...on a personal basis,' she started to defend herself.

'Yes, it has,' Daniel contradicted her flatly. 'When something arouses you emotionally your voice changes completely... I could hear the dislike and contempt in your voice quite clearly—and the fear as well,' he informed her.

When something aroused her emotionally? What about when *someone* did the same thing? Did she betray herself equally shockingly then, too?

Suddenly she was starkly conscious of Daniel's profession, of his training, of the fact that he probably knew more about people's reactions and what they meant than she could possibly know.

'What is it, Christa?' he challenged her. 'What is it about me that you find so painful, that makes you feel so antagonistic? What I am, or what I do?'

'Neither,' Christa denied quickly. Too quickly, she recognised as she watched the way his eyes narrowed, felt the full power of his concentration on her.

'I...I just don't like the idea of people being deceived...cheated...hurt.' She stumbled slightly over the words, wishing she had never got involved in such a conversation and longing to escape—but how could she do that without betraying herself even more to Daniel?

'And you think that I would do that?'

An immediate denial sprang to her lips, but somehow she suppressed it, the effort it took making her throat ache and her eyes feel gritty.

'I don't know you well enough to make that sort of judgement,' she managed to tell him shakily.

To her surprise a slight smile suddenly curled his mouth. 'You're a fighter, I'll say that for you,' he told her.

Christa stared at him. 'You *want* me to disagree with you?'

'Not exactly, but there is a certain stimulation about discussing something with someone who knows their own mind and isn't afraid to say what they think. It brings a certain kind of energy...a chemistry to the discussion, not totally unlike the very special chemistry that two people create when they're very strongly sexually attracted to one another,' Daniel told her softly.

Like someone in a trance Christa went totally still, only her eyes moving, and totally against her will they focused on Daniel's face.

'I'm not saying that I don't and won't take issue with you on what you're saying,' Daniel continued, as calmly and easily as though he had never made that reference to sexual chemistry, as though he had never left those words hanging in the air so provocatively that Christa felt as though she could still feel their echo vibrating dangerously through her whole body. 'But that kind of person, the kind of woman who negatively accepts everything she hears simply to make life easier...' He gave a small dismissive shrug.

'But men don't like women who argue with them, who are too independent,' Christa told him quickly.

'Don't they?' Daniel challenged her softly. 'That's a myth I thought was well and truly exploded. Men, intelligent men, *real* mean feel exactly the same about women who passively accept their every word as law as they do about women who passively accept their intimacy in sex.'

Christa couldn't help it; she could feel the hot, toe-curling sensation his words evoked, submerging her body in a flash-flood of intense awareness.

'Sex...making love,' Daniel continued, 'like a good discussion, should be about mutual intensity, mutual involvement...a mutual desire to share what is happening... Don't you agree...?'

'Sex for sex's sake isn't something that interests me,' Christa told him, forcing her voice to sound disparaging and curt.

'No,' he agreed. 'Nor me—call me unmacho if you like, but I really fail to see what pleasure there can be in a physical intimacy that does not include—not merely include, but also fully embrace—an emotional and intellectual intimacy as well. Which probably explains why I seem to have become unintentionally celibate...' he added ruefully.

Celibate? This man? Christa's heart lurched and floundered and then ricocheted against her chest-wall so hard that she thought Daniel must actually be able to see it beating.

'What's wrong?' she heard him asking her.

'Nothing,' Christa denied, and then added quickly, 'It's just that men...most men wouldn't say...don't tell...don't reveal their...themselves...' She stopped speaking, shaking her head beneath the onslaught of her muddled thoughts.

'Perhaps because they've learned the hard way that women don't always want to listen,' Daniel told her, apparently guessing what she had been trying to say. 'Some women find male emotions, male vulnerability, very threatening. It isn't what they've been brought up to expect from a man. Watch a small boy with his mother, observe the different way she treats him from his sister...the way society expects her to treat him. Once they get to a certain age boys are actively discouraged from being open about their emotional needs, but they do have them, and so do men.

'What are your emotional needs, Christa?' he asked her softly, catching her so totally off guard that she could only stare at him while the colour came and went in her face as she succumbed to the shock of his question.

'I...I don't want to talk about them,' she managed at last, adding fiercely, 'That isn't why I'm here...'

'No, you're here to test the efficiency of our work, on the surface at least, but there's more to it than that, isn't there, Christa? There's a personal hidden agenda in there somewhere, there inside you, something that's perhaps not quite a fear and certainly not an obsession, but something which has a very strong hold on you and no one else.'

Christa stood up abruptly.

'Stop it,' she demanded frantically. 'I don't have to listen to this, to you. I...'

'Christa...'

She almost made it to the door and to freedom, but he caught up with her just as she was reaching out to wrench it open, placing his body between her and it, catching hold of her much as he had done earlier; only this time her body, her senses, registered the subtle, telling differences in that hold, his familiarity with her height and shape, just as she knew, as she reached out her hands supposedly to fend him off, that the feel of his heartbeat beneath her palm, the heat of his skin, the faint roughness of his body-hair beneath his shirt, were something she wanted to experience again with a hunger that was already dangerous.

'I'm sorry. I'm sorry...I didn't mean to upset you. I just wanted...'

Instinctively, as she heard his softly whispered words, Christa looked up at him.

It was a fatal mistake, because her mouth went dry as she focused on his, her heart pounding frantically. The longing that engulfed her to reach up and wrap her arms around him, to press her body close to his, to pull his head down so that she could reach his mouth with her own, made her tremble with shock.

She made a soft sound of denial at the back of her throat, closing her eyes to blot out the vision in front of her. But it was no use. With her eyes closed, her other senses sharpened. She could hear the sound of his breathing, feel the rapid thud of his heartbeat.

When she opened her eyes he was looking right back at her.

'Christa.'

As he breathed her name against her mouth she gave up, acknowledging defeat, unable to fight her need any longer.

His thick, 'Open your mouth and let me kiss you properly,' sent such a violent *frission* of reaction through her that she had to cling to him for support, cling to him and do exactly what he had just begged her to do, not because he had commanded it but because her own need to experience the intimacy of his tongue exploring the inside of her mouth, stroking against her own, was much, much too strong for her to resist.

Resist... If he hadn't spoken, *she* would probably have been the one biting frantic little kisses at his mouth, silently pleading with the quick, tortured little strokes of her tongue for him to do exactly what he was doing now.

Almost delirious with arousal, Christa heard the soft, satisfied sound he made as he invited her to reciprocate his intimacy. The sensation of him sucking gently on her tongue as he drew it into his own mouth, the way his lips openly caressed hers into more intimacy than she had ever known in her life before, made her ache to feel his hands on her body, stroking it, caressing it, easing it free of the unwanted restriction of her clothes.

'God, I want you... I want you so much.'

The raw passion in Daniel's voice shocked her back to reality, panic flooding her as she felt her control slipping, her desire to respond to what he was saying, what he was asking, almost too strong for her to resist.

But she had to resist. She had to.

Her tortured, 'No,' burned her throat, her voice so low that she didn't think Daniel could possibly have heard it. But he had, and he *was* responding to it, slowly...reluctantly releasing her, his mouth twisting slightly as he watched her.

There was no way she could hide from him the fact that he had aroused her...that she had wanted him, Christa acknowledged. She was trembling so much that she could barely stand; her mouth felt swollen, bruised, too exposed to the air, when what it really wanted was renewed contact with Daniel's; when all *she* wanted...

'I'm sorry,' Daniel told her gruffly. 'I didn't intend that to happen. It wasn't planned... It was just...' He gave a small shake of his head, his voice dropping even lower as he told her, 'Things got rather out of control.'

He looked and sounded like a man who had received a deeply disturbing shock, Christa recognised, the look he gave her not only acknowledging what had happened but also appealing to her for understanding.

Emotionally as well as physically he seemed to be saying that he wanted to reach out to her...

Instantly Christa started to panic again—this time a different kind of panic from the one she had felt earlier. This panic went deeper and had its roots in mistrust, not just of him, but of herself as well.

He was lying to her, deceiving her, manipulating her. She would be a fool even to think of letting herself trust him. She didn't *want* to trust him, because once she did... He wasn't the kind of man she wanted to give her heart to...to commit herself to.

'Funny, isn't it,' Daniel was saying, his voice still slightly rough, as though he hadn't quite got himself back under control, 'how something as potentially harmless as a kiss can turn out to be so lethal? No wonder they call it sexual chemistry,' he commented in a self-derisory voice. 'That was a pretty explosive thing that happened to us...'

Immediately Christa tensed. '*Us*? There is no "us",' she told him fiercely. 'What happened was a mistake...'

'Our bodies didn't seem to think so,' Daniel interrupted her grimly. 'Far from it...'

'I...I was thinking about someone else,' Christa lied angrily. What was he trying to do to her? Force her to admit...? 'I'm not a complete fool, you know,' she told him frostily, in a last desperate attempt to reject what had happened...what she had felt. 'I'm well aware that there is a certain sort of teacher, usually a male, who sees it as a perk of the job to sexually dominate and enslave his pupils. Normally he's the type of man who isn't capable of sustaining a relationship with a woman who is his equal—his ego simply can't take it,' she added for good measure, her head lifting as she forced herself to look Daniel in the eyes.

What she saw there made her wish that she hadn't. She had never seen him looking so angry; anger to her was something that people expressed by raising their voices, making a lot of noise, using aggressive body language. But Daniel was doing none of those things.

But he was still very, very angry. She had never seen such coldness in another human being's eyes, never realised that simply the hardening of a normally warmly smiling male mouth could change a man's expression, that the cold, controlled focus of his silent fury could make tiny shivers of apprehension run down her spine.

'If you really think that that's true,' he told her quietly at last, 'then I've made an even greater error of judgement than you.'

Without giving her any chance to reply, he turned and walked over to the door.

Christa held her breath, half expecting him to stop, to turn round, to smile at her and coax her, to soften her criticism, to suggest that they discuss it as he had done on every previous occasion when she had made an angry, defensive remark to him.

But he didn't. He simply opened the door and walked through it, leaving her technically victorious in that he was the one who had walked away. But she didn't feel victorious—anything but; she felt mean and small and petty, and, which was worse, she felt as though somehow she had lost something very important. Something. Or someone.

CHAPTER FIVE

FROM her sheltered seat in the pretty, old-fashioned garden outside the farmhouse, Christa would watch Daniel working on his self-imposed task of rebuilding the dangerously unstable dry-stone wall which separated the garden from the farmland.

At first she had felt amazement and, if she was honest, even a faint sense of derision that a man of Daniel's intelligence and professional qualifications could claim to find satisfaction in such a pedestrian task. She had even said as much, but he had simply shaken his head and told her that she was wrong, that the work he was doing required skills at which he was still a mere amateur, and that there was something equally satisfying, albeit in a different way, in rebuilding the wall as there was in helping people to widen their perceptions of what life was all about and to find fulfilment outside the narrow confines of professional prestige and money imposed by modern society.

It was three days now since he had walked out of the study, leaving her on her own; three days in which he had been unfailingly polite and pleasant to her, and unfailingly distant and remote.

Leader, teacher, mentor, guru—give it whichever name you wished to choose—his attitude towards her was very strictly proper and professional. It seemed laughable now that she had ever even thought he had, never mind accused him of having, the kind of ego that needed the doting adoration of a hopelessly besotted pupil. Rather, now, he gave the impression that any attempt on her part to breach the professional distance he had created between them would be met with a courteous but very firm rejection—*very* firm rejection. Just as she would have rejected him if he had tried to introduce any kind of personal or sexual note into their relationship— wouldn't she?

She moved restlessly in her seat, uncomfortably conscious of the small, hesitant ache inside her body—an ache which had nothing whatsoever to do with the hard surface of her wooden seat or her position on it.

As she moved, she grimaced faintly as she saw the dirty mark on her trousers. Having a wardrobe which comprised only clothes in various shades of cream, camel, honey and white might, in her normal life, have been a decision which reflected not only good sense and good taste, as well as subtly displaying an almost formidably strong will, but those colours were not exactly practical for her present lifestyle!

She doubted, for instance, that the sand-washed silk shirt she was wearing now would wash anything like as easily or well as the workmanlike check shirt Daniel had on, but she wasn't the kind of woman who looked good in clothes borrowed from a man's wardrobe. She wasn't tall enough, for one thing, and for another her body was too femininely curved.

Much too femininely curved, she decided as the breeze suddenly flattened her shirt against her body, outlining her breasts.

She needn't have worried, though; another surreptitious glance in Daniel's direction showed that he was totally engrossed in what he was doing. He wasn't even facing in her direction, she acknowledged. The breeze which had flattened her shirt was tousling the thick darkness of his hair, so thick that even when it was ruffled by the wind she couldn't see his scalp. Beneath his shirt she could see the movement of his muscles as he reached out to lift another stone. Unwillingly she continued to watch him, fascinated against her will by the sheer maleness of his body, its power and strength, all the more subtly arousing for not being openly or deliberately on display.

Odd how that same flexing of male muscles by, say, a body-builder or gym bimbo, for instance, would have been a complete turn-off, whereas watching Daniel work...

Hurriedly she averted her gaze, her face flushing slightly. Her mouth had gone betrayingly dry and beneath her clothes she was discomfortingly aware of her body's awareness of him.

What was the matter with her? She had seen equally good-looking men before...dozens of them, in Milan for instance, at the biannual textile and fabric fashion fairs, and on her travels where the golden-skinned, dark-eyed good looks of some of the young men came close to classical perfection.

There was no way that Daniel was good-looking in that sense. His face was too masculine, too blunt, his jaw far too hard, his mouth far too firm... And his eyes were completely the wrong colour. Whoever heard of a man with such splinteringly clear and all-seeing eyes giving a woman the kind of long, languishing looks that stroked feather-light touches of erotic arousal over her senses? No...if she had really wanted to start having such irritating and unwanted sensual yearnings over a man there were far more suitable applicants for the post whom she could have chosen.

She frowned, trying to concentrate on the book in front of her which Daniel had given her to read. Its author's aims and views might well be very praiseworthy, but they were also impossibly idealistic in her view, and she had said as much to Daniel already.

'You know what your problem is, don't you?' he had countered. 'You cling to being a cynic because you're afraid of letting go of what, for you, has become a form of security blanket. You daren't allow yourself to trust or believe just in case you're disappointed or hurt, and so you erect a protective wall between yourself and other people.'

'Maybe I do,' Christa had agreed. 'But at least that way I'm safe...'

'Safe from what?' Daniel had probed.

'Safe from everything that happens to you when you're too gullible,' she had told him harshly.

'What things?' Daniel had asked her, but she had shaken her head, not wanting to continue what proved to be such a painful topic of conversation.

Sometimes, she felt she would never really get over her guilt at being as easily taken in by Piers as had Laura.

If she hadn't listened to him when he had told her that Laura was suffering from depression, that she was constantly accusing him of being unfaithful to her, imagining that there was another woman in his life when nothing could be further from the truth...if she had believed Laura instead and helped, perhaps her friend would have been alive today.

But it had been easier to believe Piers, good-looking, smooth-talking, deceitful Piers, rather than listen to Laura.

'Have you ever been too gullible, Christa?' he had pressed quietly.

'I don't want to talk about it,' she had told him angrily.

'So gullible and hurt that the pain has never really gone away; that it has made you determined never to trust anyone else again,' he guessed intuitively. Far too intuitively for Christa, who suddenly couldn't wait to get away from him.

'Who was he?' he had asked her quietly as she started to pick up her papers so that she could leave. 'A lover? Your first lover...'

'No. He was not my lover,' Christa had told him fiercely. 'He was my best friend's husband. He was a liar and a cheat and he broke her heart and drove her to her death. He...'

She had stopped and shaken her head, appalled at the way she was revealing so much of her life...herself to him. He had a knack of making her do that, a subtle charisma which somehow compelled her into behaviour which was surely totally alien for her.

Releasing the imprisoning side of her personality, he had called it. Freeing her to be wholly herself. But she was already herself... All the self she wanted to be.

Remembering this discussion now, Christa hunched her arms defensively around her knees and looked away from where Daniel was working towards the house. It was an attractive house, well proportioned and sturdily built, and something about it reminded her, in some odd way, of the house she had shared with her parents.

As a very young teenager she had yearned to grow up and marry, to have a large family—to replace the love and security she had lost with her parents' death.

Only a very young girl could believe in that kind of fairy-tale. Husbands did not always continue to love their wives, nor children their parents. She was far better off as she was...

'It's almost time for lunch.'

Lost in her own thoughts, Christa hadn't heard Daniel's approach, and now her body betrayed her with its shocked reaction to his proximity, her muscles tensing so fiercely that their swift contraction actually made her start to tremble.

Daniel was standing far too close to her not to be aware of what was happening to her. She could feel her face starting to overheat and quickly turned her head away from him.

'You're shivering. You should be wearing something warmer.'

He thought she was cold. She closed her eyes in brief relief, her tension easing.

'And more serviceable.'

Before she could stop him he had leaned towards her, his thumb touching the grubby mark on her trousers.

Instinctively she jerked away, unable to bear her body's reaction to his touch. Her thigh felt as though it was on fire where his thumb had rested lightly against it, and the heat from that spot seemed to throb and spread all the way over her body until it reached the most sensitive core of her being, flooding her with an aching longing so intense that she could feel her eyes starting to burn with the tears of its pain.

If Daniel were to touch her now, to hold her, to...

Out of the corner of her eye she could see the way his mouth had hardened, and her ache of longing was replaced by an equally painful sense of desolation.

'We're going to have to start walking soon. They've forecast snow for the end of next week.'

'Walking?' Christa repeated in confusion, his comment so far away from her own thoughts and feelings that it was almost as though he had spoken in a foreign language.

'Yes,' he repeated, frowning at her. 'The brochure and prospectus both explained that a very important part of our course involves a series of carefully structured mountain walks, culminating in a final walk where people form pairs and then have to make their way to a specific point with only one another to rely on.'

Now he did have Christa's attention.

'You mean you abandon them in those mountains? Isn't that dangerous...?'

'It would be if that were what we did,' Daniel agreed drily, 'but in point of fact their progress is monitored and carefully watched to make sure that they come to no harm. The purpose of the exercise isn't to frighten them but to build a sense of trust, an acknowledgement of the need to be able to trust and rely on others, to share with them.'

Christa shivered. 'But what happens if something goes wrong? If one of them gets hurt, has a fall and becomes totally reliant on his or her partner?'

'That wouldn't happen. But if it did, then the relationship they had built, the mutual sense of trust and responsibility, would ensure that the person left behind would know that his or her partner would get help.'

'I could never trust anyone so much,' Christa told him fiercely. 'Never.'

She glanced towards the mountains, thinking how terrified she would be if she were lost and alone up there, and possibly injured and unable to move into the bargain. There was no way she would be able to trust someone else to get help for her. No way at all. She would rather risk further injury by crawling on her hands and knees if she had to, by helping herself, relying on herself.

'Has it ever occurred to you that your fear of trusting anyone might have its roots in the death of your parents?'

The quiet question froze her body into rejecting immobility, her anger so intense that she was almost stammering as she threw her response back at him, demanding, 'Why should it? It wasn't their fault that they were killed, and besides, I had my great-aunt to turn to. She gave me a home...love...'

'But she wasn't your parents,' Daniel enforced quietly, 'and a child doesn't always reason as logically as an adult. As an adult you know that your parents' death was an accident outside their control. As a child, as well as a sense of loss and fear, you could also have experienced anger against them for leaving you.'

'No,' Christa denied quickly. Too quickly, she knew. How had he guessed, known about those dark feelings of bitterness and resentment she had fought so hard to suppress in the months after her parents' deaths, when she had sometimes felt she almost hated them for leaving her alone?

'And what about you?' she challenged, fighting to suppress her unwanted memories. 'According to your reasoning, you should have felt guilt at your father's death...'

Even in the heat of her anger she couldn't bring herself to be cruel enough to use the word 'suicide', not to look at him as she delivered her blow.

For a moment she thought he wasn't going to reply, and then, when he did, his answer shocked her into silence.

'Yes,' he told her, 'yes. I did... And sometimes still do. Accepting those feelings, learning to live with them instead of fighting to deny them, was one of the hardest things I've ever had to do, and the most frightening. To give up the self-inflicted punishment of those feelings, to give up making excuses to myself for all the things I didn't do because of them, was very, very hard.

'Negative emotions can be just as addictive, just as dangerous as any other kind of drug.

'Think about it,' he told her as he started to move away from her.

Christa stood up angrily, determined to refute what he had just said, and then cried out in startled pain as the wind blew dust into her eyes, causing her to blink and automatically start to rub her streaming eye.

Daniel had turned round the moment he heard her cry, hurrying quickly back to her.

'What is it? What's wrong?' he asked her.

'Nothing... Just something in my eye,' Christa told him.

'Let me see.'

'No.'

She started to move back from him, her brain already anticipating the havoc his proximity would cause to her senses, but it was already too late because he had closed the distance between them, one hand cupping her face and the other turning it slightly into the light.

Even through the pain of her watering eye, Christa was acutely conscious of the slightly rough texture of his palms and the pads of his fingers where they rested against her skin.

She shivered, her nipples peaking, bristling against the thin fabric of her silk shirt, a reaction which had nothing at all to do with being cold.

Had Daniel seen her body's betraying response to him?

'Look up...'

Instinctively she fought the calm command, blinking even more rapidly instead and rubbing her eye a second time, causing the dirt trapped against her lid to irritate the tender area even further.

Her eye flooding with tears, she tried to pull away from Daniel's constraining hold, but he wouldn't let her.

'Keep still,' he told her.

'Let go of me,' Christa demanded. 'All I need to do is blow my nose and that will get rid of it...'

'I don't think so,' Daniel corrected her. 'I can see what's causing the problem; there's some grit lodged under your lower eyelid...'

'I know that,' Christa ground out irritably. 'It's my eye—remember...'

'What we need to do is get you inside so that I can bathe it,' Daniel said to her, ignoring her childish comment. 'Try not to blink too much, if you can.'

As he released her Christa turned to face the house, and immediately cried out as the grit moved, causing her further pain.

'Don't move...'

This time she obeyed Daniel's brief command, more because she didn't have any choice than because she wanted to. With both eyes screwed tightly closed against the pain, she could hardly do anything else.

'Now lean on me,' she heard Daniel instructing her as his arm came round her, holding her firmly against the side of his body, causing her heart to miss several beats and then thud erratically against her chest wall. 'You can keep your eyes closed if that feels better. Now, let's get you into the house...'

'I can't,' Christa protested. 'I can't walk with my eyes closed.'

'You can if you lean on me,' Daniel told her. His voice sounded far too close to her ear, just as his body felt far too close to her own. She was acutely conscious of the warm weight of his arm around her, of the sound of his breathing, the scent of his skin. 'All you have to do is trust me...'

'No...'

Could he hear the sharp panic in her voice as clearly as she could herself? Christa wondered as she fought down the pain and opened her streaming eyes.

'I can manage by myself,' she told Daniel huskily.

'Maybe you can,' he agreed. 'But you aren't going to...'

Christa gasped in outraged shock as she felt him lift her bodily off the ground and into his arms. He was going to carry her into the house... Impossible. He couldn't possibly do it...

Only it seemed that he could, and with far less effort and exertion than she had expected.

It was only as he put her down in the middle of the kitchen floor that Christa suddenly realised something. She blinked experimentally and then a second time.

'It's gone,' she told him triumphantly. 'It's gone...'

'Let me see...'

Obediently she turned her face up towards him, gulping shakily as she realised just how close to him she was and that the touch of his fingertips against her face had somehow subtly changed and become far less clinical and far more... She gulped in another breath of air, her emotions suddenly in chaos. Her brain and her sense of self-preservation urged her to move away from him just as quickly as she could, while her body, her senses, her other emotions whispered yearningly to her to stay and risk the consequences.

'Have you any idea at all just how damn much I want you?' The raw, hungry demand shocked through her. The tiny circles Daniel was tracing against her skin with the pads of his thumbs were setting off a dangerous chain of sensual reaction within her body which urged her to press herself even closer against him, to close her eyes the better to absorb the sensation of his touch against her skin.

'You *can't* want me,' she protested in a papery whisper of a voice, but somehow her protest lacked conviction, and his words had already ignited a corresponding need within her, so strong that it threatened to obliterate everything else.

She did try to fight it, to cling on to rationality and reason, but she could feel the desire in Daniel's body...its strength and its hardness.

'You want me too,' he told her thickly.

'No,' Christa denied, but she knew that she was lying.

And so, obviously, did Daniel, because he ignored her protest to tell her roughly, 'And if I let my body have its way right now you'd be in my bed, in my arms, under my body, with not a damn thing to come between us but the air I'd have been fighting to breathe.

'Oh, God, don't do that,' she heard him protest in a groan as she responded instinctively to his words, moving her body against his, closing her eyes and letting what he was saying to her shiver against her skin.

'Do what?' she asked him huskily, luxuriating with feminine triumph in the knowledge of her power over him.

'You know damn well what.'

She felt Daniel's hands slide into her hair, tilting her face upwards.

'Shall I tell you what you do to me, Christa?' he whispered, a breath away from her lips. 'Shall I tell you how you make me feel ... how you make me ache?'

His hand left her face, his fingers entwining with hers as he lifted them to his mouth, slowly kissing each individual one of them and then, even more slowly, sucking on them.

Sensual shock flooded her body. She was as powerless to silence her tiny moan of pleasure as she was to stop the shudder of pleasure running through her body.

'You like that,' Daniel whispered to her. 'So do I. I love the way your skin tastes, Christa... I love its texture, its scent. And I love the way you respond to me: that soft little moan, the way your body moves against mine. I want to taste every inch of you like this,' he told her, his voice roughening and dropping even lower. 'Every inch, starting right here...' he kissed her forehead gently '...and then here...' and her mouth less gently '...and then here...' she trembled as his lips touched the base of her throat '...and then here...'

Another little moan escaped her as his fingertip traced the hard crest of one breast.

'But most of all... Most of all I want to touch and taste the real essence of you,' he told her, his voice suddenly thick and heavy with desire.

It was pointless trying to hide her awareness from him, or her reaction, her responsiveness, the physical and emotional arousal his words had caused.

I want you too, she wanted to tell him, but she couldn't quite bring herself to say the words. Instead she reached up and touched him, her mouth trembling slightly as she felt the rasp of his jaw beneath her fingertips, her touch mapping him, learning the strong contours of his face while her heart thudded a frantic tattoo of desire against her chest.

'I'd almost given up believing that I'd ever meet you, do you know that?' Daniel told her as he turned his face to kiss her fingertips. 'The woman who can make me feel like this...'

'Like what?' Christa asked huskily, her voice almost slurred, drugged, soft and creamy with the satisfaction of her atavistic feminine need to be so intensely desired.

'Like there isn't an inch of you I don't want to know. A thought, a feeling I don't want to share...a second of your life I don't want to be part of.'

'But you can't feel like that about me,' Christa protested.

'No?'

He was kissing her fingers again, but he was watching her mouth. She could feel the fierce heady excitement and anticipation start to throb through her as she held her breath, waiting, instinctively closing her eyes as she felt his hands cupping her face.

'No, don't close your eyes,' he told her. 'Don't try to hide yourself, your feelings away from me, Christa. I want to share them, just as you want to share mine.'

How could it be that the simple act of keeping your eyes open, of looking deeply into the eyes of that other person while you kissed could give such an intense degree of intimacy? An intimacy deeper even than the hungry, open-mouthed kiss they were sharing; the questing search of Daniel's tongue, the hard arousal of his body.

To look into his eyes and to allow him to look into hers when she was so emotionally vulnerable, so emotionally as well as physically aroused, was a far more intimate act than if she had stood naked before him; an act as intense and private in its way, as much an abandonment of self, requiring almost as much trust as the act of orgasm itself.

Abruptly her emotions overwhelmed her, her eyes closing, her whole body trembling as she leaned against him and whispered shakily, 'No...I can't...I...'

Immediately he seemed to understand, holding her, soothing his hand gently over her, rocking her almost as though he knew that it was comfort and reassurance she needed rather than raw sexuality.

If he could make her feel like this just by kissing her, what was it going to do to her when...? How would she feel...?

'I'm afraid,' she told him, her throat threatening to close up on the admission, her emotions pushing down her normal barriers of reticence and mistrust.

'I know. I'm afraid too.' He smiled ruefully at her as she lifted her head from his chest to look at him, but his smile disappeared as he asked her quietly, 'What is it you fear the most, Christa? The fact that I might only want sex from you, or the fact that you know I want one hell of a lot more.'

Her expression gave her away.

'I don't want to love you,' she told him wildly. 'I don't want to take that kind of risk...' She shook her head helplessly and then cried out in panic, 'I'm not ready for this...'

'Do you think I am?' Daniel asked her grimly. 'Do you think *anyone* ever is?'

'I can't go to bed with you,' she told him. 'I'm not...I haven't...I don't... We have to think about safe sex,' she finished miserably.

'I'm not asking you to go to bed with me,' Daniel told her. 'We've three more weeks of this course to go, and until then... I want things to be right between us, Christa. I want us to be able to concentrate on ourselves, each other, without any barriers between us.

'And as for safe sex...'

The look he gave her made Christa's stomach churn like a washing-machine on full spin.

'Safe sex is the last thing I want to have with you,' he told her forcefully. 'There's nothing safe about the way I feel about you, about the way I want you, and as for sex... Sex isn't what I want either. What I want from you...what I want to give you, to share with you, is just about as far removed from safe sex as it's possible to get. I want to take you in my arms and make you cry out with joy and pleasure. I want to hold you and watch you as I make you part of me in the most intimate and complete way that a man and woman can discard their separateness and come together. I want to cherish you and protect you. The delicacy of your skin, your body, stops my breath and makes me almost afraid to touch you and yet, at the same time, I want to penetrate you so deeply that your flesh will hold the memory of me within it forever. I want to wake up in the morning and see the faint bruises of my lovemaking colouring your skin. And whatever those needs are, whatever they say about me, they are most definitely not safe sex...'

'No, they aren't,' Christa agreed huskily.

No man had ever spoken to her like this before, aroused her so intensely, both emotionally and physically, simply by the sound of his voice, the message of his words.

She could actually feel the sharp, excited pulse of her own arousal deep within her body, and the need to place her hand over her stomach, her womb, where she ached physically from Daniel's explicit description of the way he wanted her, was too strong a compulsion for her to resist.

'And as for the rest of it,' Daniel continued, his voice softer, more controlled, 'I promise you there isn't anything you need to worry about. For one thing——' He paused and looked gravely at her. 'The last time I slept with a woman, I'm ashamed to say that it was more out of compassion than desire. An old friend—we were students together—who came to me for...comfort when her husband left her.'

Daniel turned his head away from her as he told her gruffly, 'She was feeling very vulnerable, all too aware of the fact that the girl her husband had left her for was many years her junior, afraid that she was no longer a sexually desirable woman. To have rejected her...'

Christa swallowed hard. She suspected from what Daniel was not telling her that he had not been the one who had instigated their intimacy. Tears momentarily blurred her eyes. What woman could resist loving such a man? Certainly not her.

'She's found someone else now and they're very happy together,' Daniel was telling her. But Christa only half heard him. She loved him. The knowledge thundered through her in a terrifying flood of emotion and need.

'And before that...before that, I had been celibate for a longer time than I like to admit...'

'Like me,' Christa heard herself saying chokily. 'In fact, to be honest, there's only been ... Well, it was just really a college thing...more curiosity than anything else and because, well, there's a certain shame to a woman's remaining a virgin after a certain age. And then I had a brief relationship with someone, but it ended when a friend of mine became...ill...'

Christa's voice trailed off and she looked away from Daniel. She and Chris had only just been about to become lovers when Laura had arrived on her doorstep, wild-eyed and in panic, claiming that her husband hated her and had only married her for her money.

Chris had resented the time she had had to spend with Laura and had claimed that her friend meant more to her than he did, and their relationship had come to an abrupt end almost before it had begun—without any real regrets on either side, Christa suspected.

'I'm not... I'm not very experienced,' she told Daniel quietly. 'Sex has never been an important motivating force in my life.'

She realised that Daniel was watching her and wondered what he was thinking, whether he was put off by the fact that she was not sexually experienced. She knew that some men would be...

'I don't suppose I should admit this,' he was saying, 'especially not in this day and age, but there's something about a woman who quite obviously isn't living the kind of lifestyle that means that she's very sexually sophisticated, a woman who has to tell a man that she isn't using a regular method of birth control, that is very sexually erotic...that makes a man feel very special...very male. Or at least that's how it makes me feel.'

The look in his eyes was making her heart do enough somersaults to guarantee its entry into the Olympics, Christa acknowledged.

Daniel was smiling at her now, the deep seriousness leaving his eyes as he teased gently, 'Somehow, I don't think that even if you could bring yourself to carry the requisite packet of condoms around with you, you'd be the type to brag about your expertise in putting them on.'

'I might not brag about it, but I certainly know how to do it,' Christa told him, blushing a little as she responded to his gentle humour. 'One of my friends' teenage daughters has told me all about it. They had a demonstration at school—with a cucumber...'

'A cucumber?' Daniel burst out laughing. 'And women wonder why men have such fragile sexual egos. Well, I think we can do better than that,' he murmured, reaching out and taking her back in his arms. 'Much, much better than that—in fact...'

'You could give me some real hands-on experience?' Christa suggested laughingly, teasing him back.

He was laughing too, but when his body suddenly hardened urgently against her the laughter died out of his eyes and out of hers.

'Three weeks,' he told her as he lowered his mouth towards hers. 'God knows how I'm ever going to wait that long. Kiss me, Christa,' he demanded thickly against her mouth, not waiting for her response, but impatiently probing her lips with his tongue instead, his arms tightening round her. The movement of his body against hers as his control slipped and the delicate exploration of his tongue became an urgent, exciting thrusting, dragging the fabric of her top and bra against her swollen nipples, already oversensitised by her desire for Daniel. The extra friction made her cry out and tense.

'What is it? What's wrong?' Daniel again said, releasing her mouth and looking down into her eyes.

Christa tried to fight the wave of hot colour that swamped her as, instead of waiting for her verbal response, he let his gaze sweep her body, intuitively coming to rest on the rounded swell of her breasts.

To her chagrin, as Christa followed his glance down her body, she could see quite plainly through her clothes the rigid and swollen outline of her nipples.

'There's no need to be embarrassed,' Daniel told her gently, correctly interpreting the reason for her flushed face and the protective movement of her arm to conceal her body. 'No, don't,' he added thickly, his hand coming up to move her arm away from her body so that he could look at her. 'I like seeing you like this ... I like knowing that you want me. Like it!' He closed his eyes briefly and groaned. 'Like it! That's just about the biggest understatement I've ever made.'

He let go of her arm and reached out and touched her breast very gently, just stroking its outer curve with his fingertips, but it was enough to send such a shock of sensation jolting through her that Christa couldn't quite suppress her small, sharp moan of pleasure.

'Do you want me to stop?' Daniel asked thickly, but even before Christa had shaken her head he was moving closer to her, his mouth leaving a burning trail of kisses against her skin, his fingers quickly working free the buttons on her shirt ... Quickly, but not nearly quickly enough, Christa acknowledged, as she arched against him with a small sob of frantic release when she finally felt the warmth of his breath against her naked breasts.

In the past the thought of having her breasts stroked and suckled by a lover had never been one she had found particularly sexually exciting, and to witness a love-scene in a film where a couple were mimicking such an act with mutual evidence of considerable enjoyment was something she had found more embarrassing than exciting. But now, with Daniel's mouth making its way down the slope of her breast while his fingers caressed its swollen peak, her need to feel his mouth against her flesh was so demandingly urgent that it literally made her feel faint with longing, her hand already lifting to press his head closer to her body, her back arching.

Her sob of relief when his mouth finally closed over her nipple quickly turned to choked, breathless whimpers of shocked pleasure as he suckled on her, slowly at first and then more deeply, more hungrily as he felt her response and her body began to move against his in an increasingly urgent rhythm that mirrored his erotic suckling.

Heat and delight radiated and pulsed from her breast all the way through her nervous system.

Low down in her body she had started to ache and soften, and when Daniel parted her legs and thrust one of his own between them she leaned eagerly against him, straining to get as close to him as she could.

Being able to feel his arousal through their clothes, knowing that he wanted her, that his body was pulsing as hungrily for her as that secret place within her own was for him, made her cry out his name in sharp frustration.

'Yes, I know. I know,' he told her thickly, releasing her breast, his face hot and damp as he leaned against her body, his hand trembling slightly as he covered the damp nakedness of her breast. 'I promised and we've got to stop. I know...'

No, that isn't what I want, Christa wanted to say, but he was already releasing her, tenderly fastening her clothes, smiling ruefully into her eyes as she lifted her head to watch him after a despairing, yearning look at the still hard tautness of his body beneath the thick covering of the jeans.

How could he do this to her, to them both when he must know how much she wanted him? Christa wondered wretchedly as he stepped back from her.

'I don't want this to be a casual, careless thing between us,' he told her gently, as though he had read her thoughts. 'Like you, I don't carry the means to ensure safe sex around with me, and once I get inside you there's just no way that I'm going to be able to stop, and the last thing I'd want...' He stopped, shaking his head, but Christa didn't need him to continue. What he meant was that the last thing he would want would be for her to conceive his child... It was, of course, the last thing she would want either, so why did hearing him say the words make her feel so much in pain?

'Anyway,' Daniel was saying as he moved away from her, 'I think it's time we moved on to less dangerous topics of conversation, don't you?

'Tomorrow we'll do our first mountain walk. Nothing too difficult, I promise. But you will need to wear proper walking clothes and boots... What is it?' he asked as Christa bit her bottom lip.

'I don't have any proper walking clothes, nor any boots,' she reminded him. 'I... The brochure...' She stopped, not wanting to lie to him, but not really wanting to admit the truth either.

'I see. Well, it isn't the end of the world. As I told you before, fortunately there's a first-rate climbing and sports equipment shop in town. We'll drive over there first thing in the morning and get you kitted out.'

As she watched him, Christa wanted nothing more than to be back in his arms, holding him and being held by him. But he was right, their personal feelings for one another had to be put on hold until after her course was over.

Which reminded her that there was something she had to say.

'Daniel,' she began quietly, holding his gaze with her own. 'This...what has happened, is happening between us won't alter my feelings about—well, it won't change my mind. I have to be honest with you. I still don't believe that what you're doing here can really...'

'The course isn't over yet,' Daniel cut in firmly. 'And don't worry, Christa, the last thing I'd expect—or want from you—is for you to let your judgement be swayed by our personal feelings.

'I'm not the kind of man who expects or wants a woman to echo my views—far from it.'

'There are men who enjoy controlling a woman through sex,' Christa pointed out quietly.

'Yes,' Daniel agreed, 'but I'm not one of them. Just as you aren't the type of woman who would want to control or manipulate a man through his desire for you.

'You know, Christa,' he added thoughtfully, 'sometimes I feel almost as though you're trying to fit me into a mould, a preconceived belief of what I am. It's as though, without knowing me, you'd already decided what kind of man I was.

'I've watched you when I've obviously said or done something that conflicts with that image. You're not sure whether you like it or not, are you? It's all right,' he told her when she remained silent. 'I'm not trying to probe or pry. If and when you want to tell me more about him, whoever he was, I'll be ready to listen. But don't judge me by him, Christa, because I'm not him.

'Which of us is it that you find the hardest to trust? Me, or yourself?'

The way he smiled at her as he reached out and gently touched her face robbed his words of any malice or criticism, but they still hurt, Christa recognised. Not just because he had so astutely recognised her feelings, but because he had also so skilfully homed in on one of her deepest fears.

She was afraid of trusting herself; of her own judgement.

She was afraid of her own feelings... Of wanting him... Of loving him, of allowing him into her life and her heart.

But it was too late, a tiny inner voice whispered to her. He was already there. She was already vulnerable...exposed and in danger...

CHAPTER SIX

'QUICK, look over there—isn't that a spaceship landing?'

Jolted out of her thoughts, not so much by what Daniel was saying as by the urgent tone of his voice, Christa looked up obediently and stared through the window of the moving Land Rover, her eyebrows lifting slightly as she heard Daniel laughing.

'Well, at least it got a response,' he defended, as she gave him a wry look. 'You've been very quiet for the last half-hour, very deep in thought. Anything I need to know about?'

The question was light enough, but the look he gave her was anything but, Christa acknowledged, and, as her heart teetered on the brink of a spectacularly high dive, her pulse-rate soared.

She had been awake half the night going over and over what had happened between them, and even when she had been asleep she had been dreaming about him. She knew how much she wanted him now, needed him, loved him, but a part of her still feared those emotions, so much so that there had been several occasions during the night when it had urged her to get up and run while she still could.

'Not really,' she fibbed now in response to his question. 'Not unless you've got a particular interest in the designs for next season's fabrics.'

She hadn't deceived him, Christa recognised, but fortunately a wandering and very reckless sheep, on its way across the road, diverted his attention for long enough

112

for her to change the subject as they turned a corner
and she saw their destination in the valley below them.

'That's the town?' she asked him unnecessarily.

'Yup.'

It looked more like a large village than a town, Christa
decided as she studied the haphazard arrangement of
narrow streets and terraced houses, grey stone buildings
set under grey slate roofs, the whole area enclosed by
the mountains which surrounded it. She could see the
open area of the cattle market to one side of the town
and, rather unexpectedly, the tall spire of a church.

'There was a time when a lot of the local landlords
were English rather than Welsh,' Daniel explained when
she commented on this. 'As well as the church, the town
boasts a posting inn and a small spa, although that's
closed at the moment for renovation.

'The slate covering the roofs was quarried locally.
There are shale deposits all over the mountains, many
of them very dangerously unstable, especially at this time
of the year when the water table can be at its highest.'

'What difference does that make?' Christa asked him
curiously.

'A great deal when there's a hidden underground water
course beneath the shale.'

They were down in the town now, its narrow streets
far more crowded than those Christa was used to. She
wouldn't have enjoyed being the one driving through
them, she acknowledged as Daniel waited good-naturedly
for people to walk past before driving on.

There was a considerable difference in attitude here
compared to her home town, she noticed, as people
stopped to acknowledge one another and call out cheerful
greetings to the drivers they made way for. At home on
a busy Saturday, drivers and pedestrians were more in-

clined to be mutual antagonists than to exhibit friendliness towards one another.

An old woman wearing a headscarf and carrying a basket was walking towards them, her face breaking into a warm smile as she saw Daniel.

He immediately stopped the Land Rover and wound down his window, calling out warmly to her.

'It's good to see you off those crutches, Meg. The ankle's mended now, has it?'

'Indeed it has,' she agreed.

'Well, just remember,' Daniel warned her, 'no more roof-mending...'

'Roof-mending?' Christa queried in astonishment when they were moving again.

'Mmm... Meg owns and runs a smallholding just outside town. Some storm damage left her without half a dozen roof-tiles and she fell and broke her ankle while she was trying to replace them.'

'What?' Christa exclaimed, aghast. 'But she must be well into her sixties...'

'She's seventy-one,' Daniel corrected her drily.

'Why on earth did she try to do that kind of job herself? Why didn't she get someone in to do it?'

'Because that isn't the way things are done around here,' Daniel told her. 'People round here are self-sufficient and proud of it. They've had to be, but in Meg's case... Well, the vegetables she grows don't bring her in much of an income and she's the kind who's too proud to ask anyone else for help.'

'But she could have been killed,' Christa protested as she tried to imagine herself even thinking of attempting to do a similar repair on her own roof.

'We'll park here,' Daniel told her, turning into a side street. 'The sports shop is only a few yards away...'

'I'm not completely helpless,' Christa told him acerbically. 'I *can* manage to walk the length of a couple of streets.'

'It's a cold day, and the wind is very sharp. You aren't dressed for that kind of weather,' Daniel told her. 'Not that you don't look good,' he added softly. 'Very good. That colour suits you... Armani, is it?' he added, indicating her suit.

Christa was surprised. The pale biscuit-coloured trouser suit was one of her favourites and it suited her, she knew, but somehow she hadn't expected Daniel to recognise its source.

'Yes, it is,' she admitted ruefully.

She was tempted to quiz him about how he was able to recognise and name the designer, but something held her back.

Why? Because she suspected... feared that it was the kind of knowledge which could only have come to him via an intimate relationship with another woman?

Piers had been very well up on all the current top designers; when he and Laura had first met he had insisted on her completely changing her image.

'He says I should only wear natural fabrics, silk and cashmere,' she had told Christa, pink-cheeked as she confessed, 'He says there's nothing more sensual than the touch of silk against a woman's skin.'

He had also been responsible for Laura having her untidy, mousy hair restyled and streaked at a top London hairdressers, and for the make-up lessons which had followed.

But none of that had apparently been enough to turn her into the woman he wanted, and it certainly hadn't stopped him from having affairs once they were married.

'Come back,' Daniel commanded quietly. 'No, I'm not going to ask,' he added, when she looked warily at him. 'When you want me to know, you'll tell me... I hope. You see, Christa, I'm not like you. I do have faith... and trust...'

Christa opened her mouth to deny his comment and then closed it again.

If only it were so easy, she reflected forlornly as Daniel climbed out of the Land Rover and came round to open her door for her, helping her out into the street.

The sports shop was a large, cheerful place, full of brightly coloured equipment and healthy-looking, smiling individuals. One of them, a girl, was demonstrating a step exercise to a slightly nervous-looking woman with two young children. Another, a young man whose muscles rippled impressively beneath his T-shirt, was walking towards them.

Christa listened silently as Daniel explained what she wanted. She was half expecting to be loaded down with thick, heavy clothing in dull colours, but the lightweight weatherproof jacket the young man produced was zingingly bright, a sharp acid yellow.

'It's a colour which can be picked out easily from the sky—a big help when it comes to mountain rescue,' Daniel told her.

Christa grimaced, thankful that that was one consideration she did not need to worry about.

Half an hour later, when they left the shop, she had bought the jacket, a pair of surprisingly fashionable protective leggings, socks, clothes, thermal underwear and, of course, boots.

'Right, now that we've got you kitted out, first thing tomorrow morning you and I are going for a walk...'

Daniel grinned at her when Christa groaned.

'Ah, there you are, Daniel...'

Both of them stopped as the old woman they had seen earlier walked towards them.

'Just wanted to thank you for what you did,' she said with a gruff shyness, ignoring Christa. 'Not that there was any need, mind. I could have managed that roof by myself... Alan Jones said there was to be no bill,' she added, giving Daniel a sharp look. 'I don't like being indebted to people...'

'One good turn deserves another, Meg,' Daniel replied easily.

'Maybe, but I haven't done you any good turns...'

'Not yet,' Daniel agreed. 'But I'm hoping that you will. It's that billy of mine; he's getting lonely. You keep goats...'

'You want me to take him off your hands? Well, I could do, I suppose...' Meg agreed. 'But I don't want charity...not even from you. I don't want others paying my way for me. I can't take him until the end of the month and you'll have to bring him over.'

'Done,' Daniel agreed with a smile. 'The end of the month it is.'

'You're getting rid of Clarence?' Christa asked him when Meg had gone. As she waited for his response she was still digesting the content of their dialogue. It was plain that Daniel had paid for Meg's roof to be repaired.

There was just no way that Piers, or indeed Daniel himself, if he had been the kind of man she had suspected him of being, would ever have undertaken such a generous act.

She could feel an odd sensation of warmth growing inside her body, an easing, a relaxing, a melting almost of some icy coldness which had previously gripped it; a feeling of relief, glorious, heady, empowering...

freeing...spread through her, making her want to smile, making her want to laugh and sing, to run, to——

'I think it's perhaps time he had a new home,' Daniel was saying in response to her question. 'He needs the company, and besides...'

'Besides what?' Christa teased him boldly, her eyes suddenly sparkling, warmth colouring her face.

'Besides, I can't have him frightening you half to death and getting you in such a state that you throw yourself into my arms,' Daniel told her softly. His eyes, she noticed breathlessly, seemed to develop an almost luminescent quality when he was happy—and aroused.

'I did *not* throw myself into your arms...' she told him in mock indignation.

'Maybe not,' he murmured. 'But that's exactly where you're going to end up any second now if you keep on looking at me like that. You do know what you're doing to me, don't you?'

'Yes,' Christa told him shakily, suddenly filled with reckless happiness.

She reached out and touched his arm, marvelling at the way even her lightest touch could affect him.

'Let's not wait, Daniel,' she told him huskily. 'I don't want to...not any more, and...and I don't think I can,' she admitted honestly.

He went so still that for a moment she thought she had said the wrong thing. The brilliance and clarity of her joy started to dim, her face flushing as she looked away from him, her voice taut with misery as she told him, 'I'm sorry... I shouldn't...'

'What? Tell me that you want me? Is that what you *really* think?'

She tensed as he took hold of her, swinging her round into the protection of a boarded-up doorway.

'Do you *know* what what you've just said has done to me? Do you *know* how it makes me feel to hear you saying something like that? Do you know how much I'm aching for you right now...how easily I could push you up against this door and...?'

The small shocked sound she made stopped him.

'I'm sorry,' he apologised, shaking his head. 'It's just... Well, last night I felt that I was the one doing all the wanting, all the feeling, all the *needing*. You seemed to have put up a barrier against me which I just couldn't get through.'

'I was afraid,' Christa admitted. She had started to tremble so much that it was impossible for Daniel not to know...not the way he was holding her.

'Oh, God,' he groaned. 'If you and I were alone right now... Perhaps it's just as well we aren't,' he added rawly as he looked at her mouth and then into her eyes. 'They serve a pretty good lunch at the Bell. Why don't I take you there and then you can order lunch for both of us while I go and do some shopping?'

Christa couldn't help it. Despite the fact that she was an adult woman who was well travelled and reasonably sophisticated, reasonably mature, she could feel her whole body flushing.

'What's wrong?' he asked her gently. 'Cold feet...?'

When she shook her head, his expression relaxed slightly.

'Good, then I shan't need to add bedsocks to my shopping-list, shall I?' he teased her before brushing his mouth lightly over hers and stepping back from her.

*   *   *

'I've ordered the beef in cider for both of us. Is that OK?'

'Fine,' Daniel confirmed as he joined Christa at the table where she had been waiting for him. He had been gone rather longer than she had expected.

'Not going to ask me what I bought?' he asked wickedly as he sat down.

Again Christa blushed.

'I love it when you do that,' he told her. 'The greengrocer was out of cucumber, by the way...'

'Stop it,' Christa commanded, almost choking on the sip of water she had taken to cool her overheated skin.

It was all so new to her, this gentle teasing, this intimacy... this loving; but she could very, very quickly grow addicted to it. Addicted to *him*, she acknowledged, as Daniel's hand reached for hers under the table.

'Mmm...this is good,' she commented when their food had been served.

'Not bad,' Daniel agreed, 'but wait until you taste...'

He stopped and watched in fascination as Christa's face suddenly turned a pretty shade of soft coral.

'Now what,' he asked her huskily, 'I wonder, caused that?'

Christa shook her head, letting her hair slide forward to conceal her flushed face from him. She had no intention of telling him. At least not at this stage in their relationship.

Her thoughts, the images his words had conjured, the desire to slowly feast herself on the banquet of his naked body, were far too personal and far too betraying for that.

'I didn't realise you could cook,' she said jerkily instead.

'Only the basics,' Daniel admitted ruefully. His eyes suddenly clouded. 'And most of those are self-taught. After my father's death ... well, my mother lost interest in normal day-to-day life. Without my father there, she seemed to lose all motivation. He was very much the centre of her life and...'

'I think most women feel like that about the men they love,' Christa suggested gently. What was it about loving someone that made you want to protect them from even the smallest pain?

Loving someone. The words still frightened her a little and she pushed them quickly away, not wanting to dwell on what they meant.

'Do they?' Daniel shook his head. 'I don't think so. Modern women have learned to be very wary of that kind of emotional dependency, to scorn it almost.'

'If we don't trust men enough to allow ourselves to be so vulnerable, perhaps that's because we've too often seen, too often experienced, men's betrayal of us...'

'That works both ways, you know,' Daniel told her, 'and in the end it all comes down to the same thing— trust, and whether you stand in line with those who give it freely or those who believe it has to be earned.'

'Let's talk about something else,' Christa begged him. The seriousness of their conversation was beginning to cloud her earlier euphoric mood. There were still vast areas of such thin ice in her newly forming relationship with Daniel which she didn't trust to bear the weight of too much intense scrutiny. Much better to skate lightly over them for now. She didn't want to dissipate the sharp sense of anticipatory excitement and desire she had felt earlier; she didn't want to risk spoiling things with too many questions. She had made her decision and now she wanted ...

She wanted Daniel, she acknowledged shakily as she glanced quickly at him. She wanted him so much that she could feel the ache of her need pulsing fiercely within her body. She didn't want to analyse the question, to wait for her doubts to return.

Totally unexpectedly, her eyes suddenly filmed with emotional tears. She put down her fork, unable to eat.

'Christa, what is it?' Daniel asked in concern. 'Is it your food—is——?'

'No,' she told him huskily as she shook her head. It's not the food...it's you, she could have said, but she just couldn't bring herself to do so. However, something in her expression must have given her away anyway, because when she added whisperingly, 'Would you mind...? Could we...could we go...?' the look Daniel gave her as he pushed his chair back and came over to her made her face burn with hot colour and her body start to shake all over.

He knew... Somehow, he knew what she was thinking...feeling.

Outside the pub she breathed in great lungfuls of the clean, cold air, trying to calm herself down. She was totally out of control, she recognised dizzily, her body, her emotions, even her thoughts no longer exclusively her own. Daniel dominated them.

He was standing next to her, watching her, his own expression sombre, but his eyes... His eyes... She closed her own, torn between shock and excitement at the message she could read in them.

Was her hunger for him as nakedly obvious in her eyes as his was for her?

The shock of recognising the intensity of his hunger— especially in a man who had previously seemed so laid-back and in control—kept her silent as they walked back to the car. As he unlocked the passenger door of the Land Rover for her, Daniel moved forward to help her into it and then stopped.

'I can't,' he told her huskily. 'If I touch you now...'

Christa had no need to ask what he meant. She already knew. She felt the same way herself, as dangerously overcombustible as brittle, dried timber, knowing that all it would take to send her up in flames was the smallest spark.

Neither of them made any attempt at conversation on the drive back to the farm. The sun was already dropping quickly towards the horizon, the sharp clearness of the sky throwing the mountains into dark, brooding relief.

It seemed impossible to believe that tomorrow she would be walking them.

Tomorrow—her heartbeat quickened. Between now and tomorrow, the present and the future, lay...tonight.

She felt more nervous, more on edge, more...more virginal than she had done when she had actually been a virgin. Her muscles tensed as Daniel drove into the farmyard and stopped the Land Rover.

When he had switched off the ignition, instead of getting out he turned towards her.

'It isn't too late. If you want to change your mind,' he told her quietly. 'Not now...not ever,' he reiterated firmly.

Christa knew what he was saying to her. Emotional tears filled her eyes.

'I haven't...I don't want to change my mind,' she assured him.

It was true, but it didn't stop her from feeling slightly afraid. Not of Daniel, but of herself, her desire, her need...her love.

While Christa collected her own shopping from the back of the Land Rover, Daniel picked up a large box of groceries he had presumably bought while she was waiting for him. Her heart suddenly started to thump very heavily and very unevenly as she remembered the look he had given her when he said he had some shopping to do.

The icy chill in the wind as they crossed the yard made her shiver, and she was glad of the warmth of the kitchen as Daniel opened the door into it.

'I'll just go and take this stuff up to my room,' she began, awkwardly, as Daniel put the groceries down on the kitchen table.

'No, not yet,' he told her quietly, taking her parcels from her and putting them down before turning back to her.

For a moment, his calm deliberateness confused her, but then he took a step towards her and opened his arms.

'Come here,' he demanded softly.

Her mouth had gone dry and her heart was somersaulting wildly.

Shakily she moved towards him, shivering with pleasure as she felt his arms close round her. As he bent his head to kiss her she could feel the fierce thud of his heartbeat. His mouth brushed hers, a fine tremor running through his body as he paused and then reluctantly lifted his mouth from hers.

'It's no good. I can't... I *daren't*,' he told her with a groan. 'I want to do this properly for you, Christa... I want to make it good for you... More than good,' he told her thickly.

'It will be,' Christa assured him, her own apprehension soothed by his male vulnerability. It made her want to reach out to him, to hold him, to tell him that she already knew that what they were going to share together would be so special that it would change the whole focus of her life. A small smile curled her mouth. He had told her before she came here that that was what he would do, but neither of them had guessed then that it would be in this particular way.

'Come and sit down,' Daniel told her, pushing her gently towards one of the chairs. 'I'm going to make us both a very special meal and then...'

'A meal?' Christa laughed. 'But we've only just had lunch...'

'A lunch which you didn't eat,' Daniel reminded her. 'Besides, isn't that what every woman wants: to be wined and dined before...?'

'She's seduced?' Christa suggested wickedly. She was feeling more confident now—now with her awareness of his own vulnerability. 'Is that what you're planning to do, Daniel—seduce me?'

She was laughing as she said it, but the laughter died from her eyes as Daniel turned round to look at her, a sharp shock of excitement burning through her veins.

'I don't need wining or dining, Daniel,' Christa told him tremulously. 'Or seducing. All I need...and all I want is you.'

She could feel her throat starting to close up with emotion as she spoke. Did he know how out of character it was for her to express her feelings so openly? Normally she was far more guarded, far more self-protective, but the way she felt about him, the way she wanted him, overwhelmed her with its intensity.

He was already coming back towards her. She stood up shakily, holding on to the back of the chair for support, her gaze fixed on Daniel's face, her heart pounding.

'Christa, Christa...' She trembled violently as he groaned her name between hungry kisses. He was holding her so tightly that she suspected she would be slightly bruised, but she didn't care. She wanted him to hold her like that. To want her like that, with the same wild intensity that she wanted him.

He was kissing her as though he couldn't get enough of her, his hands shaping her body, moulding it against his own.

'Oh, God, I want you... I want you, Christa, I want you so much...'

His hands were on her hips. She could feel the hardness of his body as intimately as she could feel the eager swell of her own breasts, the sharp, intense ache low down in the pit of her stomach, the...

She could hear a noise somewhere outside the building. It sounded like... She tensed in shocked disbelief as she heard the sound of a car engine.

Daniel had obviously heard it too, because he was already releasing her, stepping back from her, his forehead drawn into a frown.

Through the kitchen window Christa could see a Land Rover nearly as battered as Daniel's own. Its driver brought it to an abrupt, untidy halt, switching off the engine and then jumping out.

Christa recognised him immediately. It was the same man she had seen with Daniel that first evening outside the hotel.

Christa watched as he stumbled towards the door and banged urgently on it.

'I'll go...' she began, but Daniel shook his head.

'No, don't... Stay here,' he told her as he went to open the door.

Daniel's visitor looked and smelled as though he had been drinking heavily, Christa recognised in distaste as the man stumbled into the kitchen, lurching from the door towards the table and leaning heavily on it as he stared frowningly at Christa, focusing on her face with evident difficulty.

That he hadn't recognised her was obvious and Christa stiffened beneath the leering look he was giving her.

'So you're Daniel's latest, are you?' he commented drunkenly. 'Always manages to get the pick of the bunch, does our Daniel. Perhaps I ought to trade places with you,' he told Daniel, turning away from Christa. 'Earn myself some nice fat fees and plenty of eager bedmates into the bargain. You've really got a set-up here, Daniel, my friend. As much sex as you want, when you want, and you're getting paid into the bargain... God, it's got to be an improvement on what I'm getting. No sex, and an ex-wife who's doing her damnedest to screw me into the ground financially. Do you know what that bitch has done now? She's claiming that I've deliberately let the farm get run-down and she says that she's going to claim for fifty per cent of what it was worth. That was ten years ago, for God's sake. Things were different then. I got more in subsidies then than I can earn from every damn thing put together now—a hell of a lot more. She's trying to bankrupt me, the bitch. That's what she's trying to do...' He stopped speaking and turned round to peer blearily at Christa.

'What happened to that redhead you had here? She looked a real hot number... Mind you, I thought that about Alison once. She was all over me when we first met. God, she certainly had me fooled.

'You've certainly got the right idea, Daniel. Keep it short and sweet and very, very temporary... Once they get their claws into you... They threw me out of the pub, do you know that? Said I'd had too much to drink. Liars... Anyway, I thought I'd drive over here and have a drink with you. You've always been a good friend to me, Daniel... Had some rare old times together, haven't we?'

He swayed dangerously from side to side as he let go of the table and lurched across the room to where Daniel was standing.

Christa watched him with a mixture of shock and distaste, distaste for his drunken, out-of-control state, and shock because of his drunken revelations about Daniel.

Tears burned the backs of her eyes, hot and destructive as raw acid, but their pain was nothing to the pain she could feel in her heart.

It was no solace to know that she had learned the truth just in time to stop her from committing the ultimate folly, a folly which, by the sounds of it, countless numbers of other women must obviously have committed before her.

Her stomach churned nauseously as she remembered all the lies Daniel had told her, and she had been fool enough to believe him. She of all people... After all she had learned, or should have learned, from Laura's relationship with Piers.

That kind of man *always* ran true to type, she told herself savagely. There were no exceptions.

'I don't want to go home, dammit,' she heard the other man swearing angrily. 'Damn place isn't home any more... Not since that bitch left and took half the furniture with her. I want a drink...'

He was lurching towards the inner doorway, but Daniel caught hold of him and propelled him firmly towards the back door.

'I'm sorry about this,' he told Christa. 'But it looks as though our plans will have to be put on hold—temporarily...very temporarily,' he added meaningfully.

Oh, my God, how could he be so arrogantly blasé...? Didn't he *realise* that this friend had given the game away completely? He must have heard what the other man had been saying—or did he believe that she was so deeply in love with him, so desperately, physically in need of him that she would just simply ignore what she had heard?

The nauseous feeling within her stomach increased. She wanted to scream and rage at him, to cry out her pain and anguish, but pride kept her silent.

'Come on, Dai,' Daniel was saying. 'I'm going to drive you home...'

'Don't want to go home,' the other man was repeating, but Daniel was already opening the back door and almost physically manhandling him out into the yard.

Christa waited stiff and motionless until she heard the Land Rover's engine start. Even when the headlights had circled the yard then disappeared as Daniel drove away, she still didn't move.

She now knew what it meant when someone said they had been turned to stone... No, not stone, icy cold marble, her whole body heavy and old, a terrible weight that burdened and overwhelmed her—like her pain and grief.

Why, oh, why hadn't she *listened* to her logic...to her instincts? *Why* had she so stupidly given in to her emotions? The same emotions which cried out to her now to leave before they had to suffer any more pain.

Her emotions—she had made the mistake of listening to them once; she wasn't going to do so again, and besides, her pride wouldn't allow her to go. Not now.

'You wouldn't believe how long I've been celibate,' he had told her, and she, like a fool, had believed him— because she'd *wanted* to believe him. Now his words, like her love, tasted sour and bitter.

How he must have been laughing at her, mocking her. She should have *known*, she derided herself angrily.

And he hadn't even had the grace to look ashamed or embarrassed when his drunken friend had revealed the truth.

How long would he be gone? she wondered miserably as she glanced at the clock. Not that she cared, of course, she assured herself hastily. As far as she was concerned it would be a good thing if he never came back.

Angrily, she paced the kitchen, reliving the things he had said to her, marvelling at his skilled deceit. A person would actively have to enjoy lying and causing pain to be so good at it, she decided. And in her case, Daniel had really stood to score a 'double whammy', firstly in making her fall in love with him, and secondly... Because he no doubt expected that once he had her in bed, in his arms, her brain would turn to such complete mush that she would be willing to agree with anything he had to say, be it the fact that the moon was made of green cheese, or that she would be willing to publicly retract everything she had said about the centre and the business he ran.

When the tears she had tried to suppress filled her eyes, flooding them as they poured down her face, she clenched her hands into small fists and told herself to stop being even more of a fool than she already was.

The man she was crying for simply did not exist, and instead of crying she ought to be down on her knees giving thanks for Daniel's drunken friend's timely intervention, instead of...

Instead of what? she asked herself with bitter scorn. Instead of learning the truth tomorrow, or the day after... instead of having a few worthless hours of continued make-believe to taunt and torment her for the rest of her life?

How long was Daniel likely to be, and what would he do when he did return? Would he have the gall to simply ignore what had happened and assume that they could continue from where they had left off before his friend had arrived?

And what would she do, for instance, if he were to walk in now and simply take her in his arms?

She would resist him, reject him, of course. Wouldn't she?

Perhaps it might be wiser for her to go to her room, she acknowledged. An act not of cowardice or retreat, but simply of retrenchment.

CHAPTER SEVEN

WEARILY, Daniel let himself into the silent, empty kitchen. He had had to stay longer with Dai than he had planned, not merely because of his neighbour's drunken insistence on relating to him over and over again the history of the break-up of his marriage, but because of his concern for Dai's state of health.

The break-up of his marriage had hit him very badly. Despite all the apparent evidence to the contrary he had been, and in Daniel's opinion still was, desperately in love with his ex-wife. The financial problems which had resulted from their break-up were merely a focal point for the emotions the Welshman felt otherwise unable to voice; it was easier for a man of his upbringing and nature to curse his ex-wife as a money-grabbing bitch than to admit that her loss had left a gaping wound in his life that nothing was ever going to heal.

Dai's increased reliance on heavy drinking as a means of trying to anaesthetise that pain was only making matters worse; even so, his timing could have been better, Daniel acknowledged tiredly. He had tried to telephone Christa to let her know that he was going to be delayed, but when she hadn't answered the phone he had assumed that she had already gone to bed.

Her own bed...alone...when, by rights, right now she ought to have been in his bed...in his arms... A soft groan escaped past his gritted teeth. It had shocked him to discover how dangerously easily his need for her made him lose control.

132

In the past he had come to the conclusion that one of the reasons he seemed unable to fall completely and deeply in love was because he was too analytical, too much in control.

How wrong he had been, as Christa's presence in his life had proved. What he had been lacking previously hadn't been the ability to feel deeply enough on his part—just the right woman.

And Christa was that woman. He had known it immediately and instinctively, but she... He shook his head slightly.

One day soon, he hoped she would tell him what had made her so prickly and defensive and why she was so reluctant to allow herself to trust him.

His eyes clouded as he started to frown. He had always believed that mutual trust was one of the most important foundation stones of any intimate relationship, and yet here he was on the verge of making what for him and, he suspected, for Christa was a very intense and personal emotional and physical commitment, when he knew in his heart of hearts that Christa was still withholding a part of herself from him; that she did not trust him fully and completely... that she seemed, in some way, almost to want to have a reason for not trusting him—as a means of preserving an escape route from a relationship she was not really sure she wanted to commit herself to—because she sensed, and perhaps feared, the intensity of his commitment to her.

These days, many women were just as wary of giving up the independence they had fought so hard for as men had once been accused of doing, and Daniel, for one, didn't blame them, but there was no way he would ever want Christa to simply become his faithful shadow, to cease being her outspoken, feisty self, no way at all. And if he was honest it hurt him that she could think anything else.

He loved her for the woman she was. Loved her... needed her... desired her.

He closed his eyes, grinding his teeth slightly. When she had looked at him today and told him that she wanted him, that she didn't want to wait...

He knew that most people who knew him considered him to be a very controlled, laid-back type of person, not given to impetuosity or outbursts of intense passion.

If they could have seen what was going through his mind earlier on today, they would certainly have had a shock, he acknowledged grimly. He had been slightly shocked himself, and if he had given in to his feelings he would have tumbled Christa straight into the Land Rover and... Well, suffice it to say, he doubted that they would have made it back to the farm...

But that wasn't how he wanted their first time together to be. Perhaps he was being over-emotional and over-romantic, but their first time together wasn't something he wanted to rush, like fast-food snatched and gobbled down to satisfy a sharp and immediate hunger.

Making love with her, loving her, was something he wanted to take slowly and savour—a meal, to continue the food simile, in which every mouthful... He could feel his heart racing as though he had just run a steep mountain incline.

He glanced at his watch. It was just gone midnight. *Was* Christa asleep?

Quietly, he left the kitchen, making his way upstairs. Christa's bedroom door was closed. He paused outside it and then turned the handle slowly. Christa was lying on her side, her face half turned into the pillow, her hair a silky, tumbled skein of softness he longed to reach out and touch. The moonlight through the curtains bathed her exposed shoulder and arm in pale, soft light.

As he watched her, Christa moved restlessly in her sleep, her forehead creasing into a frown, dark smudges beneath her eyes as though... as though she had been crying.

Daniel caught his breath on a fierce tide of emotion and longing. Crying? For him? He ached to reach out and touch her, to wake her gently with whispered words of love and soft kisses, to watch as her eyes opened in surprise and pleasure, soft with love—and desire—but what he wanted from her went far, far beyond mere sex, beyond even a deep physical intimacy. He loved her and wanted her in his life permanently, but he wasn't so sure that she felt the same way about him. Something was holding her back, coming between them, despite what she had said to him today.

Physically she might be prepared to commit herself to him, and if Dai hadn't arrived when he had, Daniel knew that by now they would have become lovers, but Dai *had* arrived, giving him time to think and question. His original decision had been the right one, he suspected, especially if he was right in thinking that part of the reason for the ambiguity of Christa's feelings for him lay in her antagonism towards his work.

Better to wait until the course and everything that went with it was behind them before...

If he could manage to control himself for that long. Well, at least tomorrow shouldn't prove too difficult to get through, he acknowledged ruefully, as his glance was caught by the boots Christa had purchased earlier. They would be out on the mountain for a good part of the day.

It was ironic that he would be conducting an exercise designed to promote and reward mutual trust and dependence on a one-to-one basis with the one woman he wanted, above all other people, to trust him and the one woman whom he suspected did not.

Very, very gently he bent down and brushed the lightest of kisses over her bare shoulder... the very lightest of kisses. Even so, as he straightened up, the tension in his body was so fierce, so intense, that he could feel his muscles shuddering under the impact of forcing it down.

In his heart of hearts he knew that, no matter what Christa might say, no matter what she might believe, she felt she was still not ready to give him the wholehearted commitment and trust that he wanted. And no matter how good the sex between them was—and he knew already that it would be good for him—without that commitment and trust it could never be enough.

'Are you sure you're all right?'

Angrily Christa turned away from Daniel, her fingers curling tensely round the mug of hot coffee she was drinking. How dared he sound so—so... caring and concerned... so genuine, when she knew—and he must know that she knew—just how much of a fabrication his supposed concern really was?

'Of course I'm all right,' Christa lied tersely, still avoiding looking at him. 'Why shouldn't I be?' she added challengingly.

Last night had been bad enough, hurtful enough, but waking up this morning had been like waking into a nightmare.

'I'm sorry... about last night... I did ring but you must have gone to bed,' Daniel had told her when she had finally forced herself to go downstairs.

She had shaken her head over his question about what she wanted for her breakfast.

'You must have something,' he had insisted. 'We've got a long day ahead of us and lunch will only be hot soup and a sandwich. Once we get out on to the mountain you'll find you need every ounce of energy you can muster.'

'Yes, I suppose I must, mustn't I?' she had agreed acidly.

It had been on the tip of Christa's tongue to tell him in no uncertain terms that she was staying exactly where she was, but caution had prevailed. At least walking would give her something to do other than brood over her unhappiness, her misery and her hurt.

Hurt. Such a small word to describe such an enormity of pain.

She didn't know how Daniel had the sheer gall to behave as though nothing had happened, watching her with that cheating, cruel pretence of caring in his eyes, when all the time——

'I thought you said you wanted an early start,' she reminded him coldly now, finishing her coffee and getting up but firmly keeping her back towards him so that she didn't have to look at his face, his eyes . . . his mouth.

Oh, dear God, please don't let those tears she could feel burning so treacherously behind her eyes dare start to fall and betray her.

'Christa . . .'

'I'll go and get my stuff on,' she told him stonily, ignoring him.

Half an hour later, when she came back downstairs, her heart felt even heavier than the boots on her feet. Much, much heavier.

Alongside her anger and bitterness ran a frightening thread of panic and pain. Despite what she now knew about him, a part of her was terrified that she might not be strong enough to do what she knew she had to do; that her emotions, her love, might defeat and betray her. She couldn't look at Daniel without remembering how it had felt to be held in his arms, without a part of her still achingly wanting to be there, to ignore the truth and make believe that he hadn't lied to her, had meant all those things he had said to her.

She was afraid of her own vulnerability, she recognised, as she turned away to avoid meeting the questioning, frowning scrutiny Daniel was giving her.

'Come over here and sit down,' he commanded, catching her off guard and gently pushing her down into a chair before she could resist.

When he knelt on the floor at her feet, for one heart-stopping moment she thought he was actually going to throw himself on her mercy and beg for her forgiveness, and, as she looked down at his dark, downbent head and the unexpected vulnerability of his exposed nape, she ached with love and longing for him.

His hands were encircling her ankle, moving her foot within her new boot.

'These laces aren't fastened quite tightly enough,' he told her.

Her boots... He was checking up to see if she had fastened her boots properly. A semi-hysterical bubble of mock laughter forced its way into her throat at the contrast between the prosaic reality of his intentions and her fantasy imaginings.

'And you mustn't leave the laces trailing like that,' he added, deftly untying them and tightening them before quickly re-tying them for her. 'You could trip over them and fall.'

'Thank you.' Christa spat the words out as though they were grit. As Daniel lifted his head to look at her she could see the questioning scrutiny in his eyes, but she refused to respond to it. Why the *hell* didn't he take his damned hands away from her body?

If he kept on holding her ankle in that ridiculously theatrical pseudo-loverlike grip, stroking his thumb against the inside of her ankle as though he just couldn't resist the need to touch her, she was going to have to tell him exactly what she thought of him. Either that, or... She just managed to suppress her small betraying gasp as her body responded treacherously to him, quivering shocks of pleasure making her tremble so openly that she had to jerk herself free of his constraining grip.

As they left the farm and headed for the track which led up into the mountains, Christa tried not to think about how things might have been if only they had not been interrupted. Would they have still been doing this this morning, or would they still be in bed together, their bodies entwined in sensual warmth?

'Are you sure you're all right?' Daniel asked her, turning round to wait for her to catch up with him. 'Earlier you looked pale; now you look very flushed.'

'I'm fine,' Christa lied for the second time.

To the untrained eye—*her* eye, Christa admitted unwillingly—the path Daniel had taken climbed slowly and easily up the lower slopes of the mountainside, but her body, and in particular her legs, had a different opinion. She was not a fitness fanatic but she had always enjoyed walking and did so regularly, often choosing to do so in preference to using her car. Her kind of walking, though, bore no resemblance to what she was doing now. It wasn't just her anger and pain that were responsible for her monosyllabic responses to Daniel's easy conversation.

Not only were her legs aching; her lungs were beginning to feel the strain as well.

A surreptitious glance at her watch told her that they had only been walking for a couple of hours and that it was barely eleven o'clock. Daniel had said they would rest for lunch at twelve-thirty and then start to make their way back.

'You're doing very well,' she heard Daniel tell her warmly. 'Most of our first-timers protest that they've had enough at this stage.'

Did they, indeed? Stoically Christa gritted her teeth, firmly trying to ignore the agonised messages from her protesting calf muscles.

'If you do want a rest, there's a good place to stop a few yards on, where you can get an excellent view of the farm and...'

'I don't want to stop,' Christa told him fiercely. 'I just want to get this whole charade over and done with...'

She bit angrily into her lip as Daniel stopped walking and stood in front of her, forcibly stopping her as well.

'Look, something *is* wrong,' he told her quietly. 'Don't, please don't deny it... If it's because of last night...'

'*If*...' Christa exploded, unable to hold back her anger any longer. '*If*... How could there be any "if" about it?' she blazed furiously. 'How could...?'

'Look, I understand... I was...disappointed as well...' Daniel interrupted her.

'Disappointed...' Christa stared at his face, her whole body flushing with mortified colour as she realised what he was implying. 'My God, your arrogance is just unbelievable,' she told him. She laughed with bitter wildness. 'Disappointed about what, Daniel...? Disappointed about missing out on going to bed with you? And what a wonderful experience that would have been for me, wouldn't it? Wonderful but, of course, hardly unique... Not for me. And not for all the other gullible fools who've been deceived and lured into your bed before me...'

'Christa, what...?'

She could hear the shock and bewilderment in his voice, see them in his face, and with them too she could see his pain... *His* pain...

'The game's over, Daniel,' she warned him. 'There isn't any point in bothering to lie to me any more. Not now that Dai has given the game away. No wonder his wife left him if he's been trying to model himself on you. What was it he said about you? Oh, yes, I remember now, he said he envied you your string of conquests and the opportunities your business gave you to add to them—and to add to your bank balance at the same time.' Christa's voice dripped sarcasm as she threw the words at him, pride and anger driving her on through the pain which had buried its cruel talons in her heart.

'Christa, no...' she heard Daniel protesting. 'Please listen to me. You misunderstood——'

'Misunderstood?' Christa interrupted him acidly. 'Oh, no, Daniel. You're the one who's done that. Not that you're the only one to blame...' Her mouth curled in a bitter humourless smile. 'After all, it wasn't as though I didn't know what type you were, how little you could be trusted... I should have listened to what my brain was telling me instead of——'

'How little I could be trusted?' Daniel questioned her sadly. 'Or how little *you* wanted to trust me. Christa, what Dai said has no bearing whatsoever on the reality of my life; it's simply his interpretation, his fantasy if you like, of the way he believes he would live were he in my shoes—a means of asserting his manhood, of restoring his faith in his masculinity.'

Christa's mouth had suddenly gone very dry, her voice an angry whisper as she demanded, 'If that's the truth, then why didn't you say something at the time; why did you let him...?'

'Because it simply never occurred to me that you'd give the slightest credence to what he was saying. Because I assumed that you'd see his comments for what they were—the pathetic and sad ramblings of a drunken man suffering from the hurt of losing his wife. What Dai was saying has so little resemblance to the reality of *us* that it never even crossed my mind that you'd take him seriously,' he told her quietly.

Christa felt sick and dizzy from the wild chaos of her thoughts. He was lying. He had to be.

'I can't make you believe me, Christa...just as I can't make you trust me, and that's what all this boils down to, isn't it? Trust...' As he spoke, he took a step towards her, and immediately Christa panicked. Another few steps and he would be touching her, holding her, and once he did...

'No, don't,' she told him, quickly stepping back from him. 'Don't come any closer, don't touch me...'

'Christa, keep still...don't move...'

As she heard his sharp warning Christa panicked— she had already taken another step backwards...into nothing, falling so heavily down the concave shale-covered slope where the mountainside fell away sharply from the path that she was too shocked even to cry out, falling, sliding, rolling in the avalanche of shale-dust and noise which had overwhelmed her, bruising her, choking her.

Terrified, disjointed thoughts flashed through her brain as she was carried swiftly down the steep slope. Daniel telling her how dangerously unstable the shale could be. Daniel pointing out to her the steepness of the mountainside and the depth of the narrow ravine into which the mountain fell.

Dust choked her nostrils and filled her eyes. The tiny pattering of the moving shale had become a low, menacing roar. She screamed as all the breath was driven abruptly out of her body as she collided with something solid.

'Christa, Christa...'

Dazed with shock and pain, she realised that her fall had been broken by a large boulder perched precariously on the edge of a narrow shelf of semi-solid slate jutting out of the mountainside.

She was lying on her side and, while every part of her body ached and throbbed, unbelievably, nothing seemed to be broken.

As she struggled to sit up she heard Daniel calling out urgently from above her.

'No, Christa, don't move... Just keep as still as you can.' Keep as still as she could! Why? What was going to happen? The ledge she was on was very narrow. Below it she could see the steep fall of the mountainside before it disappeared into the ravine.

She started to tremble violently, her imagination far too readily conjuring up images of what would happen to her if her frail sanctuary should collapse. *Was* it her imagination—when she moved, did the slate actually move as well?

'I'm going to have to go and get help,' she heard Daniel saying. 'While I'm gone, you must try to keep as still as you can...'

'No...' Christa's denial was a scream of pure terror. 'No, Daniel. Don't leave me here...please stay with me...'

She was trembling and sobbing, filled with panic and fear at the thought of Daniel walking away from her, at the thought of being left alone here on this narrow, fragile piece of slate which could so easily give way beneath her... Daniel was doing this to punish her; he was going to walk away and leave her...leave her on her own to die...to die alone... He wasn't going to get help at all. He was...

'Christa, I *have* to go. I have to get help, but I promise you, if you just listen to me and do as I say, you will be safe. Listen to me, Christa... Trust me...'

Trust him... A sob of pure hysteria bubbled in her throat. If she had trusted him in the first place she wouldn't be here now. Trust him? How could she? How could she allow herself to be that vulnerable? How could she open herself to that kind of risk...that kind of pain?

He could walk away from her right now and leave her here. No one would ever know. He could simply say that there'd been an accident... He could...

'Christa, promise me that you'll do as I say...that you won't try to move...'

How had he guessed that that was what she was already planning? She'd already decided that the moment he had gone she was going to try—she had no idea how—to somehow or other get herself back on firm ground...

'Promise me...'

Promise him. Trust him!

She bit her lip to suppress a frantic sob...

'I can't,' she told him fiercely. 'I can't...'

'Then I can't leave you,' she heard Daniel saying above her. 'And since I can't rescue you without help, that only leaves us with one alternative...'

Christa's heart missed a beat. He was going to leave her. He was going to walk away and leave her here on her own.

'I can't save you, Christa... but at least I can die with you...'

Die with her... Christa tilted her head and saw Daniel crouching down on the mountainside above her, starting to make his way down to her...

'Daniel, no...'

The sound was torn from her throat, an anguished protest that revealed her true feelings.

He was prepared to die with her.

'I'll do what you say,' she told him, tearfully. 'I'll stay here. I won't move... I promise.'

'Christa?'

Dizzily Christa lifted her head and opened her eyes. It seemed a lifetime since Daniel had left her to go for help. At first she had felt strong and brave, buoyed up by the emotional impact of knowing that he had been prepared to sacrifice himself to be with her, but gradually that euphoria had seeped away and in its place had come panic and fear, the temptation to move, to try something, anything to escape so strong that she had come dangerously close to giving in to it.

But she had promised Daniel, given him her word. Tears clogged her throat. What if, after all, he had been lying to her throughout?

'Christa...' She tensed as she heard Daniel calling her name a second time.

Drifting in and out of a state of semi-shock, at first when she heard Daniel calling her name she thought she must be imagining it, and doggedly refused to give in to the temptation to look upwards. A small flurry of displaced shale rattled past her, causing her to tense her body in panic.

'Christa...'

This time she knew she was not imagining it, even if the sound of Daniel's voice was coming, not from above, but from behind her.

Cautiously she turned her head and looked sideways, her heart flooding with joy and tremulous disbelief as she saw Daniel slowly and painstakingly making his way down the steep mountainside towards her, supported by a rope secured around his body, his downward progress agonisingly slow.

Christa could see now why he had told her not to move. Each careful toe-hold he managed to gain in the shale disturbed its own small avalanche of loose flint, tiny trickles of moving mountainside running together into rivulets which were already gathering force, combining together, increasing in speed.

Crouching tensely on her narrow ledge watching him, Christa wasn't aware of the tears flowing down her face, making clean tracks in the dust coating her skin, until Daniel arrived alongside her and told her huskily,

'It's all right now, Christa... Don't cry, my love. Everything's going to be all right. The Air Sea Rescue people are sending a helicopter to pick us up ... it should be here soon ...'

Carefully, he eased his way on to the ledge beside her.

A helicopter... Automatically Christa glanced upwards along the route he had just descended and, although she didn't say anything, Daniel obviously realised what she was thinking.

'It's too much of a risk,' he told her gently.

Too much of a risk... but *he* had taken that risk to be with her. Her heart turned over achingly, fresh tears squeezing from her eyes to run helplessly down her face.

'It's all right... it's all right,' Daniel repeated, moving closer to her, reaching out his arm to draw her closer to him.

He felt warm and safe, the scent of his skin preciously familiar. There wasn't room on the ledge for Christa to do what she wanted to do, which was to throw herself into his arms and beg him to hold her tightly. The ledge was barely wide enough for her body as it was, and Daniel was crouched half on and half off it, supporting himself partially on the metal spikes he had driven into the shale.

'Trust me', he had said, and, alone on the mountainside waiting for his return against all odds, somehow in the deepest part of herself she had known that she could, that he simply wasn't the kind of man who would walk away and leave anyone suffering or in danger.

And if she could trust him with her life, surely she could trust him with her heart... with her love?

'You shouldn't have come down here,' she whispered shakily to him. 'You shouldn't have taken such a risk...'

'I wanted to be with you,' he told her simply, his hand reaching out for hers, his fingers interlocking warmly with her cold ones as he gave them a comforting squeeze. 'This is hardly what I'd got planned for us for today,' he told her wryly.

'No?' Christa responded, trying to match his attempt at lightheartedness. 'And there I was thinking it was all part of your master plan to convince me of the efficiency of your courses: mutual trust, mutual dependency...'

Fresh tears filled her eyes.

'And you shouldn't be here. You shouldn't have taken such a risk. It's all my fault...'

'No, it's mine,' Daniel corrected her gravely. 'I knew this morning that something was wrong, but I thought...'

'That I was sulking because of last night...'

A spasm of pain crossed her face, her skin losing all its colour, causing Daniel to demand anxiously, 'What is it? What's wrong?'

'Nothing,' Christa told him. 'It's just...' She lifted her head and looked at him. 'Oh, Daniel, if anything happens to us...to you... We've never even been lovers. I've never felt your skin next to mine. Never touched you and held you... I was thinking about that before you came back. Thinking about how stupid I've been...how much time I've wasted. You were right, I didn't want to trust you. I *was* afraid.'

Shakily she explained to him what had happened to her friend Laura. When she had finished, he was so quiet that at first she thought he was angry with her.

'I know I shouldn't have stereotyped you,' she told him huskily. 'And I know you were right when you said that my fear of trusting anyone probably goes back to losing my parents... Please don't hate me, Daniel.'

'Hate you?'

His voice sounded rough, as though he had swallowed some of the dust raised by the shale.

'Oh, my God, Christa. If I was going to hate anyone it wouldn't be you; it would be myself... I should have given you more time... more understanding, instead of arrogantly demanding that you give me your trust...' He stopped speaking, frowning and turning his head to look upwards.

'Listen,' he demanded. 'That's the helicopter. Can you hear it?'

Christa could—just...

'It will soon be over now,' he promised her, 'and when it is...' The look he was giving her made Christa's body tingle all the way up from her toes to the top of her head. 'When it is, I'm going to make sure that you make good all those sweet, sexy promises you've made to me.

'And there's going to be interest on every single one of them!' he warned her throatily, 'At compound rates...'

'Sounds as if I'll have to spend the rest of my life in bed with you working off the debt,' Christa responded, giddy not just with the relief of knowing they were going to be rescued but also with the unfamiliar weightless, light-hearted feeling which she recognised came from unburdening herself to him and, for the first time in her life, sharing with someone her most deep-seated fears.

She felt almost drunk on the relief of it, euphoric, and so light-headed that she could almost have floated back up the mountainside.

'Oh, Daniel...' Her heart was overflowing with emotion as she reached out and gently touched his face.

'Don't,' he groaned. 'The helicopter will be here any minute and the last thing I need is to go down in history as the first man to get turned on by being trapped halfway down a mountainside. We all know that danger can be erotic, but not to this extent.'

Christa tried to reply but the helicopter was virtually overhead now, the sound of its engines drowning out anything she might have tried to say.

With the arrival of the helicopter and the rescue crew, things happened so quickly that in retrospect Christa could only remember them as a confused blur; the mixture of sickening fear and relief she felt when she was finally winched up into the safety of the helicopter combined with her anxiety for Daniel, who still waited below her, was certainly something she would never forget, nor was the small scrap of conversation she suspected she was not intended to overhear between Daniel and the winchman when they were finally both on board and the helicopter was heading back to its base.

'Your directions were spot on,' she heard the winchman saying to Daniel. 'Just as well; there's a heavy bank of cloud moving in from the coast pretty fast and if we'd had to waste time looking for you, you could have ended up spending the night out there. You're damn lucky you weren't any higher up; exposure kills more climbers than falls. And what the hell possessed you to go down there? You're on one of the local search and rescue teams; I don't need to tell you how bloody treacherous that shale is. The whole mountainside could have gone—it's happened before.

'It's only a couple of years back that a whole party of experienced climbers, five of them, were all lost in a similar incident.

'At least the girl was reasonably safe, although I wouldn't have wanted to trust myself too long to that ledge, but you... If that shale had started to move...'

'It was a calculated risk,' Daniel responded quietly, so quietly that Christa had trouble straining to listen to what he was saying.

'Rubbish,' the winchman contradicted him graphically. 'There are only two things that could make a man take that kind of risk...one of them is that he's that kind of man, pure and simple...a risk-taker and, as far as we're concerned, a pain in the neck...the type that gets off on playing at being a hero; and then there's the other type...the type of man who's never done a fool-hardy thing in his life, who knows the risk but takes it anyway out of love.' He paused, giving Daniel a thoughtful look as Christa felt the hot, healing tears flood her eyes.

Daniel loved her, and she shouldn't have needed to hear someone else say it to know that. No matter what happened between them in the future, no matter that Daniel, because of the sheer generosity of his nature, would forgive her for doubting her, a part of her would never forgive herself; a part of her would always regret that she had not had the courage, the faith to believe in him.

Reluctantly, Christa opened her eyes, her heart pounding with fright until she realised that she was not, after all, still on the mountainside but safe in bed in the farmhouse.

Despite her protests that she felt fine, the hospital had insisted on giving her a thorough check before releasing her into Daniel's care, with the strict injunction that she was to stay in bed.

That milky drink he had given her had to have had something more in it than mere cocoa, she decided wryly now, as she registered the heavy lethargy of her body and brain.

Daniel...

As though she had actually called his name, the bedroom door opened and he came in, the sombreness leaving his mouth and eyes as he saw that she was awake.

'How are you feeling?' he asked her as he came over to the bed.

'As if I've just gone ten rounds with a grizzly bear,' she responded jokingly.

'Try substituting ten tons of shale for the bear,' Daniel suggested drily.

He had insisted on remaining with her in Casualty after they had cut off her protective clothing.

'They're only surface abrasions, that's all,' the nurse had assured him comfortingly when she had seen his face. 'They look worse than they actually are and they'll soon heal.'

Surface abrasions or not, there had been something about her bruised, lacerated skin that had made him want to take hold of her and wrap her protectively in his arms; that had made him ache to take their pain into his own flesh in the same way that he already carried his guilt for what had happened.

Trust me... Promise me, he had begged her, and yet he had known as he walked away from her that her safety lay far more in fate's hands than his own. Who knew how far back into the precarious shale that small shelf of slate went? And yet he had also known that he had no option other than to leave her and go and get help.

'What time is it?' Christa asked him prosaically.

'Almost six-thirty,' he told her.

'Six-thirty?' Christa sat upright in bed and winced as her bruises made their presence felt. 'That means I've been asleep for almost twenty-four hours.'

'Actually, it's closer to eighteen,' Daniel told her, not adding that he had gone without sleep for almost an equal length of time, terrified of even closing his eyes in case she needed him.

'Well, that's still nine hours too long—by anyone's reckoning,' Christa replied spiritedly, 'and I'm getting up.

'I'm hungry,' she added plaintively when she saw that Daniel was about to protest. 'I didn't get any dinner last night—nor the night before...'

Silently they looked at one another, the look they were exchanging saying more than any words.

'I don't want to be here on my own, Daniel,' Christa told him huskily. 'I want to be with you. We came so close to losing one another...and I don't just mean because of my fall...'

'Don't,' Daniel groaned in protest, reaching out to cover her hand with his. His, Christa noticed, was trembling slightly. 'I'll never forgive myself for what happened.'

'You must,' Christa told him. 'It was just as much my fault as yours. More... If I had only trusted you. I'll never doubt you again, Daniel. Never, I promise...'

She leaned towards him slightly, her glance dropping from his eyes to his mouth.

'Oh, God, Christa.'

Daniel kissed her with careful hesitancy, as though she was as fragile as a brittle piece of china, Christa recognised.

As he released her she looked wistfully at his mouth. How did you tell a man that, despite your cuts and bruises, you ached so badly for him that you'd willingly add quite a few more to your collection just for the pleasure of being held in his arms and made love to with all the intensity and passion of his earlier verbal promises?

Not easily, she recognised, as Daniel moved away from the bed.

'I'll leave you to get dressed. I've got a couple of telephone calls to make...'

As he opened her bedroom door, Daniel cursed himself under his breath. No wonder Christa had been looking at him with that mixture of bewilderment and hurt in her lovely eyes. But if he had stayed with her a moment longer, bruises or not, there'd have been no way he could have stopped himself joining her in bed and giving thanks, not just for their safety, but for the resolution of the problems and barriers between them, by making love to her. Wasn't that one of woman's most heartfelt complaints against their men: that they persisted in showing their emotions through the physical act of sex? And yet to do so was one of the most basic and deep-rooted of male drives and instincts.

He had seen the bruises on Christa's body. If he touched her now, held her, *kissed* her, there was no way he was going to be able to be as gentle and restrained as she needed him to be. Even kissing her so briefly just now, he had had to fight to hold back the urge to crush his mouth down on hers, her body beneath his.

He had never dreamed he could be the victim of such primeval instincts and needs. He had never come even close to feeling anything like this before—but then he'd never been in love before.

* * *

Christa frowned as she walked into the silent, empty kitchen. It had taken her longer to shower and dress than she had anticipated, her arms aching by the time she had shampooed and dried her hair, to such an extent that, instead of dressing properly as she had planned, she had simply pulled on a big, loose, soft shirt. It covered her from throat to knees, after all, the pale triangle of the cotton briefs she had on beneath it barely visible. And if it was possible—just—to make out the dark areolae of her nipples against the paler flesh of her breasts, well, surely she and Daniel had now reached a stage in their relationship, had a degree of intimacy between them which, even if they were not actually as yet lovers, meant that he would understand that her mode of dress had nothing to do with enticement or provocation; that her fall had affected her more physically than she had wanted to admit.

Where *was* Daniel, though? She opened the kitchen door and walked back into the hallway. His study door was open and she could see a light on inside the room. Calling out his name, she pushed open the door and walked inside, stopping abruptly as she saw him. He was seated in his chair—fast asleep.

A wave of love and tenderness rolled over her as she watched him. Impulsively she walked over to him, dropping down on her knees beside him, saying his name softly.

He muttered something in his sleep but didn't wake up properly. The light from the fire played across his face, revealing its strong bone-structure. Christa reached out and touched him, tenderly tracing the shape of his face. Love and longing filled her, along with a deep sense of gratitude to fate and to Daniel himself.

A less tolerant, less understanding man would not have been so patient with her, so... so caring. Daniel had a strength which she suspected few other men could match. She could depend on him utterly, she recognised, trust herself to him completely and without reservation.

Hot tears filled her eyes as she slowly leaned forward and gently kissed his mouth.

The first few buttons of his shirt were unfastened and she slid her hand inside it, taking comfort from the warmth of his flesh against her palm, the steady rise and fall of his chest as she leaned her head against it. It felt so right being here with him like this. *He* felt so right.

Lovingly she stroked the strong column of his throat with her fingertips and then replaced them with her mouth, a caress which began as a tribute to him as a very special human being, but which changed with deceptive speed to something far more intense and sensual as her body suddenly registered its desire for him and its reaction to the scent and taste of him.

Helplessly Christa surrendered to the need pulsing through her, her lips clinging to the warmth of his skin as she caressed first his throat and then his shoulder, her hands impatiently pushing aside the barrier of his shirt as she drank in the scent of him and moved closer to him, her own shirt dragging against her body, exerting a brief pressure on her breasts that made them ache sensitively for the firmer stimulation of Daniel's hands.

Christa shuddered deeply, her eyes closing as she visualised him touching her, removing her shirt and then cupping her breasts lovingly in his hands, his eyes looking deeply into hers as he slowly stroked the sensitive peaks of her nipples. She could feel the heat and desire her own thoughts were generating right down deep, down within her body.

Shocked by it, she instinctively sought to subdue it, pressing herself closer to Daniel, steadying herself by placing a supporting hand on his thigh, an instinctive and unthinking action, unplanned and automatic; but when her fingertips relayed to her the information that even in sleep Daniel's body was aware of her, it wasn't shock that made her fingertips linger for a startled heartbeat on the rigid swell beneath his jeans.

The ache within her body intensified as she fought down the temptation to run her fingertips caressingly over him—and not just her fingertips, she acknowledged as her heartbeat alternated between a fast, dizzy racing and a slower heavier thud.

Bemused by the unfamiliar extent of her own sensuality, she didn't even realise what she was doing with the hand she had lifted from his thigh until the shirt she had unfastened fell away from her body, revealing the swollen firmness of her breasts and the silky sheen of her skin.

Slowly she unfastened the buttons of Daniel's shirt as well, breathing in sharply as she studied the bronzed strength of his chest, with its soft arrowing of dark hair. She touched it experimentally, marvelling at the combination of hard, warm flesh and soft, silky hair and then, helpless with longing for him, she leaned forward, burying her face against him, breathing in the scent of him, slowly kissing her way up over his breastbone until she reached his throat, until the swollen peaks of her breasts were only a breath away from the naked warmth of his chest.

All she had to do was to release the breath held pent up in her lungs and the gap between them would be closed.

A small frantic moan bubbled in her throat as she suppressed the desire to rub herself against him, the need to feel his flesh, his body, against hers. Quickly she kissed his throat instead, tracing the line of his jaw, the shape of his mouth... his sleep-closed eyes.

Only his eyes weren't closed any more.

Embarrassed, guilty heat poured through her body as she suddenly realised what she was doing.

'When... when did you wake up?' she asked him in a suffocated, faltering voice.

'Am I awake?' Daniel groaned. 'I thought I must be dreaming.' He saw her flushed face and reached out and touched her cheekbone with one finger. 'Don't be embarrassed,' he told her huskily. 'I can't think of a more sensual compliment a woman could pay a man than the one you've just paid me.'

In her embarrassment Christa had already started to lift her body away from him, but Daniel's hands on her arm stopped her, his thighs closing around her, trapping her.

Christa trembled as she saw the way he was looking at her, his study of her slow and heart-rockingly sensual as he took his time, his glance lingering for so long on her mouth that she gave a small erotic shiver, nervously wetting her lips with the tip of her tongue, but that was nothing to the sensation that poured through her as he fixed his attention on her breasts.

'I didn't mean... I just wanted... I never...' she began to stammer, her whole body beginning to burn with the heat of the way he was looking at her, of her own knowledge of just what his concentrated study of her was doing to her.

'You don't have to apologise, Christa... or explain,' he told her softly as he lowered his head towards her body. 'If you feel for me just one tenth of the need I feel for you right now...'

Christa gasped out aloud, her whole body arching in sensual shock as his lips closed delicately over one nipple. She had fantasised about him caressing her like this, but the fantasy came nowhere near being anything like the reality.

With his hands splayed across her back, under her shirt, supporting her, Christa found herself arching back in an almost pagan pose of abandonment to the unbearably erotic movement of his mouth against her body.

The firelight highlighted the creamy paleness of her body, threw into relief the outline of her breasts and the darkness of Daniel's head against them.

When she cried out in sharp, high arousal, he released her nipple gently. Christa shuddered as she looked down at her body and saw the damp gleam of her own sensually transformed flesh.

A fine sensual shudder rippled through her body, as though it had been touched by the lightest breath of air. In the pressure of Daniel's hands against her skin she could feel the fiercely controlled force of his naked desire; see it in the glitter of his eyes.

'Oh, God, Christa,' Daniel moaned as he leaned forward, his face hot and damp against her skin as he pressed his open mouth against her belly, his tongue circling her navel. 'I want you...I want all of you,' he told her throatily as his hands slid to her thighs.

'No, Daniel. Wait... Please...there is something... Take off your jeans,' she whispered shakily, her colour mounting as he lifted his head and looked at her, her words shocking her almost as much as they had evidently surprised him; but there was no recalling them now, and besides...

'I want to see you, Daniel,' she told him. 'I want to touch you, to...' Hesitantly she reached out and let her fingertips rest lightly against his jeans-clad thigh. She trembled visibly, wondering if she had gone too far, if the complete stillness of Daniel's body meant that he was turned off by her almost aggressive sensuality. She had never felt like this before, never experienced any desire to touch a man, caress him as she was doing now with Daniel.

'Please...' she begged achingly, her whole body suffused with colour and heat.

'You're supposed to be resting,' Daniel protested, but she could see from his eyes what her whispered plea was doing to him, and when he reached for his zip his hand was trembling almost as much as hers had done.

He undressed quickly, almost matter-of-factly, without either embarrassment or vanity, accepting her silent study of him with its uniquely feminine blend of bold anticipation and shy, tender awe. Only once did he hesitate, pausing to look at her and say gruffly, 'I thought I knew all there was to know about being a man, about my own sexuality, but the way you're looking at me right now...'

Christa could see in his eyes his love for her. It removed the last of her defensive barriers, her voice catching with emotion as she told him bravely, 'You're so beautiful, Daniel.'

'Beautiful? Oh, Christa...' His body shook slightly as he laughed ruefully. 'Now I know why they say love is blind.'

'Not blind,' Christa assured him. 'Just the opposite, in fact, and you *are* beautiful to me, Daniel. Inwardly as well as outwardly... I would still love you for the person you are even if you didn't look like this,' she told him quietly, huskily, her eyes blurring slightly with tears as she leaned forward and gently kissed the inside of his thigh.

'Christa...'

She heard the warning in his voice—and ignored it— as the desire she had kept so carefully controlled suddenly erupted hotly inside her, and, by the time Daniel had lifted her to her feet, standing up with his arms wrapped tightly around her, her body pressed close to his, silencing her soft protests with the urgent, passionate demand of his mouth, she was openly trembling with the force of her need for him.

She couldn't remember discarding either her shirt or her briefs, only the mind-destroying pleasure of Daniel's mouth as it touched her skin, her throat, her breasts, the soft, smooth skin of her waist and stomach and then moving lower.

She shuddered violently as she looked downwards and saw his dark head pressed against her body, her fingers reaching out to tighten convulsively in his dark hair as his fingers gently parted the soft protective folds of her womanhood. She could feel the warmth of his breath against the most intimate part of her body as he touched her gently with his tongue, and her whole body started to shake.

Never, never in her whole life had she experienced such an intensity of sensation, such an awareness of being loved and desired.

She could hear Daniel whispering to her between caresses that the taste of her was the sweetest thing he had ever known, that it was the ambrosia and nectar and the elixir of life itself all rolled into one, and that for the rest of his life he would be so helplessly addicted to the taste of her that there would be no life for him without her.

When he finally gave in to her husky imploring and lifted her up to carry her over to the fire, where he laid her down in the impromptu nest of cushions he had made for her, she could taste her own body in his kiss.

'Daniel, I want you so much,' she told him. 'I want you.' Her back arched, her soft cry of pleasure as she felt him entering her lost beneath the fierce pressure of a kiss that mimicked the slow thrust of his body within her own.

There had never been any pleasure like this, could never be any pleasure like this, she thought deliriously as her body closed possessively around him, so sensitive to him that each and every movement he made sent a fresh paroxysm of pleasure spinning through her.

The sensation which had begun with the moist pressure of his mouth against her breasts, which had grown and flowered with the intimate caress of his tongue against the most sensitive part of her womanhood, now began again, flowering into a vast explosion of exquisite pleasure, so intense that, as she cried out Daniel's name, her eyes filled with emotional tears.

'Look at me,' Daniel had commanded as he'd entered her, and the intimacy of their shared deep eye-contact had, in its way, been even more intimate than the physical joining of their bodies.

As he reached out and touched her tear-damp face, Daniel's eyes were dark with awe and emotion.

'I knew it was going to be good between us,' he told her rawly. 'But this . . . you . . . You made me feel that I was almost immortal.' He smoothed the damp hair back off her face and bent his head to kiss her gently and then far more lingeringly.

'Daniel,' Christa told him shakily. 'Tonight I want to be with you . . . to sleep with you . . .' Her eyes searched his face, looking for some sign of hesitation, of rejection, but there was none.

'Do you honestly think there's any chance of my letting you do anything else?' Daniel demanded roughly as he took hold of her hand and raised it, palm upwards, to his lips. 'If you think I'm going to be happy letting you get more than an arm's length away from me from now on——'

He let go of her and ran his fingertips gently up her arm, causing her to shiver in soft pleasure.

'There is one problem, though,' he told her frowningly. Uncertainly Christa looked at him. What was he going to tell her...? That he didn't want her permanently in his life? That when he said he loved her he didn't mean that he would love her forever...? That...?

'Yes...what...?' she demanded, dry-mouthed with anxious tension.

'That safe sex we discussed practising,' Daniel told her sombrely. 'Well, we didn't, did we?'

It took several seconds for his meaning to sink in and, when it had, Christa flushed guiltily. 'That was my fault. I...I wanted you too much to...to wait or——'

'No, it wasn't your fault,' Daniel corrected her. 'The responsibility was mine and I should have, but once I'd tasted the sweetness of you and felt your body's responsiveness to me...the last thing I wanted was anything, anything at all, coming between me and that sweet sensitivity.

'But, if there should be consequences——'

'Consequences,' Christa interrupted him uncertainly.

'Yes,' Daniel confirmed, his hand hovering over her soft, femininely rounded belly. 'If you should have conceived my child, Christa, it will mean marriage. Both you and I know how important security is to a child, how much they need and crave the security of knowing that their parents, both their parents, will always be there for them.'

'M-marriage?' Christa stammered, staring at him. 'But...'

'Perhaps we should take the precaution of going ahead and getting married anyway...' Daniel continued.

'You'd do that? Marry me...just in case I were pregnant...?'

'I'd marry you tomorrow,' Daniel told her hoarsely, 'given half the chance, and whether we'd been practising safe sex or not, that's the way I feel about you, Christa...the way I want you...totally and permanently. But I know it's too soon for you to make that kind of commitment. Two days ago you didn't even believe you could trust me to be honest with you...'

She *had* hurt him with her refusal to believe in him, Christa acknowledged as she wrapped her arms tightly around him and held him.

But she would never hurt him again—never!

CHAPTER EIGHT

'ARE you awake?'

'No,' Christa fibbed, snuggling closer to Daniel's warm naked body and nuzzling her face into the curve of his shoulder, smiling as he groaned and protested.

'If you keep wriggling up against me like that you know what's going to happen, don't you?'

'No,' she denied mock innocently. 'Why don't you show me?'

But the teasing laughter died out of her eyes as Daniel took her at her word and started oh, so slowly and erotically caressing her body while he whispered in her ear exactly what he was going to do to her and what she was already doing to him.

'Daniel, no,' she protested huskily as her body started to respond to his arousal. 'You said you wanted an early start this morning, remember?'

'Yes, but that was before,' he told her, his voice muffled by the soft weight of her breast as he gently closed his lips around her already taut nipple.

'Before what?' Christa demanded, her own voice equally husky.

'Before I remembered that there are far, far more important things in life than work,' Daniel responded. 'Far, far more important.'

Sighing voluptuously, Christa stopped arguing with him. After all, there was nothing she would rather do than lie here in Daniel's arms.

This fortnight or more had passed with frightening speed, she acknowledged as she ran her fingers down Daniel's spine, closing her eyes in silent pleasure at the sensation of his skin beneath her fingertips and her awareness of the effect she was having on him.

Another three days and it would be time for her to leave, to return to her own life.

'I can't let you leave,' Daniel had protested the previous night after supper as she lay curled up on the settee beside him watching a television documentary. 'I want you here with me for always, Christa...'

'I have to go,' she had told him. 'There's my work...and the house...'

'You can work from here,' Daniel had told her, shaking his head as he saw her expression. 'All right, I know. You need time. Perhaps I shouldn't have been so careful about ensuring that you didn't conceive these last few nights and instead...'

'Oh, Daniel,' Christa had protested, 'it isn't that I don't want to stay with you!'

'Just that you aren't ready to commit yourself to marriage with me yet,' he had suggested.

'It's such a big step to take. I know I love you...but the life you lead here...your work...' She paused, shaking her head, not wanting to hurt him but compelled to be honest. 'I know how deeply you feel about what you're doing here, Daniel. But I'm not sure I can feel the same way...be so committed...'

'I'm not asking you to be,' had been his surprising response. 'After all, you don't expect me to get excited over a new fabric pattern, do you? I don't *want* to change you, Christa. That isn't what loving someone is all about...'

'But when I came here you said you would change the way I felt,' Christa reminded him. 'I do feel different, Daniel, in that I accept that your belief in what you're doing is genuine and heartfelt, but...'

'But part of you still doesn't wholly trust me,' Daniel had concluded for her sadly.

'*No*. It isn't that,' Christa had denied. 'Of course I trust you... How could I not, after what you did...after the way we've been together? No, it isn't *you* I don't trust, Daniel...it's just that I can't...'

'You can't quite let go of the past,' Daniel finished for her. 'You can't quite let go of your fear that I might turn out to be like your friend's husband. Christa, dishonesty is something that comes from within the person themselves; it isn't a product of the way they earn their living.'

'No. But——'

'But what? There are certain stereotypes that must always be true...?'

Christa had shaken her head, unable to say anything. They hadn't actively quarrelled, but that night the shadow of what had been said had lain between them in bed, and even though Daniel had made love to her with his normal passion and intensity, she had been conscious of a slight withdrawal in him, and within herself a small painful sense of something having been lost.

'I've got to go,' she reiterated now. 'I'm due to fly out to Pakistan the day I go back. I've got meetings planned that I can't cancel...' She closed her eyes and told him achingly, 'Oh, Daniel, I'm going to miss you so much. I want to be here with you, I want it more than anything else in the world...'

'*But*...' he finished for her. Sadly Christa watched him.

'We don't have to rush things,' she told him, half pleadingly.

'No, we don't have to,' Daniel agreed, 'and yes, there are a hundred or more good reasons why we should be sensible and take things slowly, but that isn't what all this is about, is it?

'You're still holding back from me, Christa. From us...'

'No, that isn't true,' she denied, but she knew that it was.

It wasn't that she didn't love him—far from it. It wasn't even, any more, that she didn't trust him, not, at least, in the sense of knowing that he would never hurt her, that he would always put her emotional and physical safety first.

But there was still, deep within her, a sense of wariness about the centre and about his work. If she was honest with herself, if he had still been working as a lecturer... But it was the man she loved, she told herself insistently, not what he did.

When Daniel talked with passion and enthusiasm about his future plans, about the benefits of what he was trying to do, all she could see was the other side of the coin, the false hopes and vain, glorious boasts Piers had made, the people he had hurt.

It wasn't that she didn't want to be with Daniel. She did, desperately so, but at the same time she was afraid; afraid that it just wasn't possible for him to be as wonderful as he seemed; that he must have a hidden flaw which would destroy her happiness.

She *was* still afraid, she acknowledged, afraid of committing herself to him, afraid of being hurt.

'I wish I weren't going to Pakistan,' she said contradictorily now. 'I'm going to miss you so much...'

Daniel smiled gently at her as he kissed her, but he didn't suggest that she cancel her trip.

'It will only be for three weeks,' he said instead.

Three weeks. Christa closed her eyes. Right now, if he was out of her sight for three hours she started suffering from withdrawal symptoms.

When she and Daniel were together like this, locked in the intimate privacy of their own special world, nothing else seemed to matter. It seemed impossible for anything to come between them.

'Loving one another doesn't mean that we have to feel exactly the same about every single issue, you know,' Daniel told her gently now. 'We're human beings. There are bound to be times when we think and feel differently about things.'

'Some things,' Christa agreed. 'I just wish...'

She stopped. What did she wish? That things were different? That Daniel were different? No, never that.

'I just need time, Daniel,' she told him. 'Everything's happened so quickly.' But she couldn't quite bring herself to meet his eyes, and when he kissed her she could sense the pain she was causing him.

In three days' time her course would be over and she would be going back to her own life; by this time next week she would be in Pakistan negotiating with her suppliers, bartering with them over the cost and terms of next year's fabrics.

At some point before she left, Daniel was going to ask her if her time here with him had wrought the life-transforming miracle he had promised. What could she say to him? That her love for him had certainly transformed *her*, but that she remained as unconvinced as ever that his courses offered anything more than some escapist game-playing for those involved in them?

As she blinked back hot tears she turned to him, wrapping her arms around him as tightly as she could while she closed her eyes on her pain.

The skin of his back felt silky-warm against her palms, its texture, like the shape of his body, the smell of his skin, the sounds he made when he loved her, the way he moved, everything about him, having become heart-wrenchingly familiar to her during this last precious week.

Familiarity, far from decreasing the intensity of her love and desire, had only fed it, so that now merely the act of running her fingertips caressingly down his spine was enough to stir her body into quick arousal.

When she kissed him, tracing the hard line of his collarbone, she heard him moan softly under his breath, his hands sliding up over her body, cupping her breasts gently, caressing her already hard nipples. When he gathered her up against him, slowly drawing her nipple into his mouth, bathing it in the moist caressing heat that instantaneously turned her bones to liquid, his hands slid to her thighs, stroking the shaping of the firm outer flesh and then more urgently stroking her soft inner skin.

Her body was already eager and waiting for him, her quick moans of pleasure joining the other sounds of their lovemaking; the silken stroke of skin against skin, the slow suckle of Daniel's mouth, the urgency of the low groan of pleasure he gave when she touched him intimately, closing her fingers around his flesh and caressing him, not just with desire, but with tenderness and love as well. He was so vulnerable to her when he was like this, so much in need, the words he whispered to her, as well as the movement of his body, openly showing the depth and intensity of his love for her.

The feel and sight of his maleness fascinated her. This degree of intimacy with a man was unfamiliar to her, and something about the way he watched her when she looked at him and touched him made her feel a soft, aching tenderness for him that deepened her love.

Now, as she lifted her head to caress him lovingly with her lips, it wasn't just desire that motivated her but a need to show him how much he meant to her. The fulfilment of every male fantasy, she acknowledged drily: woman worshipping at the fount of man's most essential maleness; only she knew that Daniel would never misinterpret so insensitively what she was doing. He simply wasn't that sort of man. Fresh tears filled her eyes. Why *couldn't* she banish that small, final shadow of doubt? Why couldn't she simply accept his choice of the way he earned his living instead of——?

As her tears dampened his thigh, Daniel reached down for her, lifting her against his body, cupping her face as he looked down into her sad eyes.

'Oh, Christa,' he groaned. 'You don't know how tempted I am to make it impossible for you ever to leave me. To keep you here ...'

'How?' Christa asked him. 'Barefoot and pregnant...' She tried to smile, to make the words light and teasing, but her voice wobbled dangerously and she saw from Daniel's expression that he was not deceived.

'Don't tempt me,' he warned her rawly. 'Don't tempt me...'

And perhaps the saddest thing of all, Christa acknowledged an hour later as she lay drowsily in his arms, was that a part of her almost wished that he would take the initiative from her and make her stay; that he would make for her the decision which she could not make for herself.

* * *

Christa frowned as she heard someone ringing her front doorbell. She had only returned home a couple of hours ago, and after dropping her off and seeing her safely inside Daniel had announced that he had a business appointment with the head of the town's Chamber of Commerce.

'But I'll be back as soon as I can,' he had told her. 'We still have to say goodbye properly...'

Christa had flushed a little, wondering how both of them were going to fit in her small single bed and at the same time wishing that it were possible for Daniel to stay the night with her, and that she didn't have to leave so quickly for her early evening flight to Pakistan.

'You'll get in touch with me...when I come back...?' she had asked him shakily, dreading now the moment of parting.

'I'll be waiting on the doorstep for you,' Daniel had told her.

Her pulse-rate quickened expectantly as she rushed to open the door, but it wasn't Daniel who was standing outside, it was Paul Thompson.

As Christa stared at him, he smiled his wide shark's smile at her, his small eyes flickering over her body. He really was loathsome, Christa decided; how he managed to be able to claim so many sexual conquests she really had no idea.

'I heard you were back,' he told her, walking into the hallway before she could stop him. 'Your new friend is down at the Town Hall now.' He shook his head in mock sadness. 'I really am disappointed in you, Christa. You've never struck me as the kind of woman who'd be stupid enough to fall for a man like that. He's already telling everyone that your retraction is as good as in the bag. Good in bed, was he? He must have been, I suppose... Pity. If I'd known what you were looking for, I would have obliged myself,' he added insultingly. 'He's made a real fool of you, you know, Christa,' he told her tauntingly. 'They'll be sniggering over your downfall at the next chamber meeting once they find out how easily he conned you into his bed. It's the oldest trick in the book, you know.'

Paul Thompson had left the front door open and out of the corner of her eye Christa saw the Land Rover pull up outside and Daniel get out.

Relief flooded through her, melting the icy coldness of the shock which had paralysed her as she listened to Paul Thompson's venomous comments.

'He's made it obvious to everyone that you and he were lovers,' Paul continued sneeringly, 'and so it's no secret how he got you to change your mind. You do *know* why he did it, don't you? There's a nice fat contract in it for him—profit along with pleasure...now that's what I call an astute businessman.

'You should have questioned him a bit more closely, Christa, instead of being stupid enough to trust him,' Paul was telling her tauntingly, oblivious to Daniel's silent presence behind him.

'I don't...' Christa began angrily, and then stopped as Paul sensed Daniel's presence behind him and turned round.

He had enjoyed bullying and tormenting her, but he was nothing like so brave when confronted with Daniel, Christa recognised as she watched him gaping at Daniel before scuttling and half running past him in his urgency to escape.

'He came to tell me...' Christa began, but Daniel cut her off, saying curtly,

'I heard what he came to tell you.'

Reaction was beginning to set in, Christa recognised, as her body started to shake. Her lips were trembling so much she had to clamp them shut, but along with her shock and disgust at what Paul Thompson had been saying there was also a heady, almost buoyant sense of relief... of release. Because when she had been listening to the venom and spite spewing from Paul Thompson's mouth, she had suddenly known, indubitably and unequivocally, that there was no way that Daniel would ever have said any of the things Paul had taken such enjoyment in repeating to her.

How Paul knew about their relationship she had no idea, but what she did know was that Daniel, her Daniel, would never, in any circumstances, boast about using any kind of underhand means to achieve any kind of objective—not with her... not with anyone, because he simply wasn't capable of that kind of behaviour.

I don't believe you—that was what she had been about to tell him, that was what she had known and felt.

'Daniel...'

She turned towards him to tell him what she had discovered, how she had felt, but he ignored her, his mouth hard and compressed as he told her bitterly, 'Nothing's really changed, has it? You still won't let go of those barriers of yours. You still, deep down inside that cold little heart of yours, want to reject me. Well, for your information, everything he told you was a pack of lies. I did tell the head of the Chamber of Commerce about our... relationship, but purely because I felt I owed it to him to explain why I had to withdraw from the promise I had made him with regard to changing your mind about the centre's work; but that was all I told him.

'But you needn't worry, Christa. I understand how important this need of yours to distrust me is... How very, very much more important than... anything I can give you.

'When I told you that for me trust is one of the most important cornerstones of any worthwhile relationship, that was exactly what I meant. You don't trust me, Christa, and I doubt that you ever will.'

He turned away from her and walked back through the still open door.

'Daniel,' Christa protested when she realised that he was actually going to walk away from her... that he was leaving her. But it was too late, he was already halfway to the Land Rover, quickly outstripping her as she ran to catch up with him, firing the vehicle's engine and driving off without even giving her a backward glance. Leaving her standing alone on the pavement, too shocked to cry. She was beyond that... beyond everything, blessedly anaesthetised from the pain she knew was to come by the enormity of what had happened.

She tried to find him, ringing round every hotel in town and finally, in desperation, the head of the Chamber of Commerce at home. But no one knew where he was.

Three hours later, white-faced with pain and grief, she rang the farmhouse from the airport, clinging desperately to the receiver as she prayed for him to answer.

They were already calling her flight. She ached not to have to go, but the discipline instilled in her by her aunt was too strong for her to ignore.

She would ring him from Karachi. Talk to him... Explain...

CHAPTER NINE

CHRISTA'S flight arrived late in Karachi and the monsoon had arrived early. She had to fight her way past other travellers, porters and baggage, and then wait twenty minutes in a queue to use the phone—all in vain; there was no reply from Daniel's number.

Fighting back the tears threatening to overwhelm her, she went outside to hail a cab.

The hotel was the one she always used when she visited Karachi, but, despite the fact that she had confirmation of her booking, she discovered that they did not have a room for her.

'I am so sorry,' the pretty receptionist apologised sincerely, 'but we have a big party here from one of the Gulf states and they have taken over the whole floor. I can ring round and see if I can get you a room elsewhere, if you wish.'

Wearily, Christa nodded her head. Half an hour later the girl confirmed that she had found her a room—at a hotel she had never heard of on the other side of the city.

When she finally reached it she discovered that the hotel was considerably older than the one she had originally booked into, with no fax facilities and no telephone in her room.

Hyped up on emotional stress and jet-lag, Christa paced her bedroom floor, mentally composing a letter to send to Daniel, closing her eyes on a small sob of anguish when she acknowledged that all she wanted to say to him needed to be said in person.

She couldn't blame him for reacting the way he had, but if only he had stopped and let her explain that he had jumped to the wrong conclusion and that, far from giving any credence to what Paul Thompson had told her, she had been about to tell the other man that she knew that there was no way that Daniel would ever have behaved in such a way.

Her rejection of Paul's allegations had been instinctive and immediate; it hadn't required thought or consideration.

So why, oh, why, when she had known so immediately and instinctively that Paul Thompson was lying, had she not been able to give Daniel the complete trust she knew he had wanted before?

Why had she held on so tightly to her stubborn dislike of his chosen way of life? Dislike—or jealousy?

She stopped her pacing and stared unseeingly at the wall.

When she had originally lost her parents and been given a home with her great-aunt, the latter had explained to her that she had a business to run and that Christa must understand how important that business was.

Then, Christa had been too young to recognise the very warm heart her great-aunt kept hidden beneath her slightly stern exterior, and certainly too young to understand how very, very hard it had been for a woman of her great-aunt's age and upbringing to take over the family business and make her way in what was, then, very much a man's world.

She had thought her great-aunt was telling her that the business was far more important than she was, not understanding that the older woman was concerned about how she was going to manage to bring up her orphaned great-niece and continue to earn enough money to support them both as well.

She had, in those days, seen the business as her rival, Christa acknowledged. Of course, later she had come to understand and see the true position and to appreciate just how difficult things must have been for her great-aunt when she had first come into her life.

And that initial jealousy had become a dim memory over the years. Something to smile at a little when she looked back on her younger self.

But, like the death of her parents and her subsequent subconscious belief that they had somehow deserted her, and that consequently anyone she came to love might do the same thing, perhaps that jealousy had left a far deeper mark on her psyche than she had realised.

Daniel was very much involved in his work. He believed very deeply in its benefits and it was an area of his life that, through her choice, she could not share.

Did she, then, perhaps subconsciously see it as a rival, a threat to her own relationship with him, something which might ultimately take him away from her...be more important to him than she was? And was it perhaps her jealousy which had been motivating her in her rejection of his way of life?

Was she, perhaps at some subconscious and yet childish level, attempting to dispose of her 'rival' by making him choose between them and then telling herself that, unless he could put her first, his love wasn't worth having?

Deep in thought, she started to frown. It wasn't either pleasant or easy facing up to such a facet of her personality. In fact, her instinctive reaction was one of shocked rejection.

She would never do anything so manipulative. It simply wasn't in her nature... Not in her mature, adult nature, perhaps, she acknowledged, and certainly never in any premeditated way, but, subconsciously, might not the child within her...? Oh, Daniel—if only he were with her now. If only she could explain, talk to him.

Suddenly she was filled with an imperative urge, not only to correct his misinterpretation of what he had overheard, but also to discuss with him what she felt she had discovered about herself.

The relief of discovering why she had been so afraid of trust and commitment, and the pain of not having Daniel there to share it with her, brought the soft sting of hot tears to her eyes.

If only she could just close her eyes and, by some magical means, transport herself back to Wales, to the farmhouse, to Daniel's arms.

She tried to ring him one more time before she went to bed, but once again there was no answer.

During the night the heaviness of the monsoon rains caused minor flooding on the outskirts of the city and damage to the telephone system, which meant that, when Christa woke up in the morning, not only could she not telephone Daniel, she couldn't get in touch with any of her suppliers either.

A day spent dashing from one appointment to another, and trying to keep her thoughts clear enough of Daniel to try to concentrate, not only on examining the samples of fabric she was being shown, but also on keeping firmly in control of her negotiations with Karachi's astute cotton traders, left her feeling as exhausted mentally as the heat and damp of the monsoon was doing physically.

When she returned to her hotel at the end of the day, her hair and her clothes were clinging stickily to her skin. But, much as she longed for the cool refreshment of a long shower, the first thing she did was to rush to the phone.

The disappointment that flooded her as she realised that it still wasn't working was sickeningly acute.

Today, studying the fabric samples she was being shown, she had known that her mind was not on what she was doing. The fierce exhilaration she normally felt on first seeing the new designs simply hadn't been there. She might as well have been looking at a piece of sacking, she recognised hollowly.

Oh, Daniel... Where *was* he? What was he doing? Was he thinking about her, missing her...wanting her...?

The way he had stormed off like that had been so out of character; he was not an irritable, easily angered man. Far from it. Of the two of them, she was the one who was the most impulsive... the more volatile.

Oh, Daniel!

She sat down on her bed, her eyes blurring with tears.

The days dragged by, long-drawn-out hours of misery and anguish, despite all the work she had to do. The telephone systems were repaired, but the telephone at the farmhouse still continued to ring emptily into the silence.

She was taken round factories, shown a vast array of fabric samples, taken out to dinner, wined and dined and flirted with, but the real essence of her simply wasn't there, she acknowledged tiredly when the morning of her departure finally arrived.

The longing to be back at home which had coloured her first few days in Pakistan had now gone. Instead, she was almost dreading her return home. While she was here it was still possible—just—for her to play 'let's pretend' and kid herself that everything was all right. That Daniel had not walked off and left her; that everything was still as it had been before they left Wales. That she was going home to him…to his love…to their future together.

But, now that she was about to go home, that comforting fiction could no longer be maintained. She was dreading her arrival in Britain, she acknowledged, dreading having to face up to the reality of having lost Daniel's love.

And she *must* have lost it, otherwise…surely he would have been in touch with her?

At Karachi airport she discovered that there had been a mix-up with the tickets and that her flight was overbooked. An apologetic official promised her that they would put her on standby and give her the first vacant seat available.

Eighteen hours later, when she finally climbed on board the flight for Manchester, Christa wasn't sure whether the nausea and cramps that were making her feel so ill were caused by a bug she had picked up or by the nervous tension of her delayed return. As she shook her pale face in rejection of the meal the stewardess was offering, fighting down the queasy nausea which had persisted all through the flight, the woman seated next to her grimaced sympathetically and confided, 'I know what it's like; I was sick the whole of the first six months with my first. Morning sickness! That's a joke… I was throwing up morning, noon and night, twenty-four hours a day, every day... Still it was worth it—in the end,' she added with a smile.

Stunned, Christa stared at her. Pregnant... Her... Oh, no... Impossible—she couldn't be... Could she?

'If there are any consequences it will mean marriage,' Daniel had told her. But that had been then, and this was now.

The woman could be wrong, of course. She might not be pregnant.

But what if she was, what would Daniel say...? Do...?

By the time the plane landed at Manchester airport, Christa was both physically and mentally exhausted.

She had, she reflected tiredly, been through every permutation of what her possible pregnancy could mean during the long flight home, and the stark truth stalked her like a silent enemy as she made her way through Customs.

If Daniel insisted on marrying her because she was pregnant, she would never truly know if he had done so out of duty rather than out of love, and he would never know if she had lied to him when she told him that he now had her complete trust. The baby, *their* baby, their *child* would be burdened by their mutual inability to be completely open and honest with one another, when it should have been born into a world of love and joy.

By the time she was through Customs she had made up her mind. She was not going to tell Daniel that she was pregnant, not just for his sake but for their child's as well.

Lost in the slow pain of her own thoughts, she would have walked straight past the solitary figure standing watching the weary travellers trudging towards the exits if he hadn't suddenly called out her name.

'Daniel!' She stared at him in open disbelief.

He looked tired and grim, his eyes slightly bloodshot, his jaw rough with shadowy stubble.

'Thank God you're all right,' Daniel told her hoarsely as he relieved her of her luggage and took hold of her arm. 'I've been trying to ring you but the hotel had no record of you booking in, and then when you weren't on your flight...'

He was holding her, Christa recognised, as though he was determined never—ever—to let her go.

'There was a problem with the hotel room,' Christa told him dizzily, suddenly beginning to feel oddly light-headed.

Daniel was here. He had come to meet her. He had tried to contact her...

'I tried to ring you,' she told him, 'but you were never there...'

'No, I've been up at Dai's farm. He collapsed with alcohol poisoning the night you left and I've been staying up there trying to keep things going.

'Christa...'

'Daniel...'

They both stopped and looked at one another.

'Daniel,' Christa began shakily again, her heart over-flowing with love and the joy of knowing that he still cared; that she mattered enough to him for him to be here, that...

'No,' he denied her softly, 'let me speak first—please...'

Emotionally Christa watched him. Once she had explained to him just how wrong he had been in suspecting that she had been going to tell Paul Thompson she did not trust him, then she intended to make sure that he knew, irrevocably and for all time, just what it had meant to her to see him waiting for her here and to see his love for her in his eyes.

'I love you, Christa,' he told her fiercely, 'and if it makes me less of a man to admit that I need you more than I need my pride, then so be it. I'm not going to pretend that your trust isn't——'

'Daniel, don't,' Christa begged huskily. 'I do trust you... I realised that when I was listening to Paul Thompson spouting all that rubbish about you telling people that you'd taken me to bed to get me to change my mind about your courses. It was so obvious that it couldn't possibly be true,' she added scornfully, her voice softening slightly as she said, '*That* was what I was going to say to him when you walked in. Ridiculous, isn't it,' she added, her voice becoming dangerously wobbly, 'that it took listening to someone like Paul to make me see the truth? I was jealous of your business, of your enthusiasm for it. I was afraid that somehow it would come between us.'

'Nothing, nothing could ever do that,' Daniel assured her roughly. 'You're my life, Christa, my love... my soul...'

As she listened to him, Christa felt her bones starting to melt, her body beginning to ache.

'Don't look at me like that,' Daniel warned her hoarsely. 'Not here in public. Have you any idea what it's been like—not knowing where you were? How you were... I've spent the last eighteen hours checking the passengers on every flight from Pakistan...'

'There had been a mix-up over the booking and I had to wait for a standby seat,' Christa told him. 'Oh, Daniel...'

As they stood facing one another, gazing into each other's eyes, someone bumped into Daniel, apologising as he hurried past.

The forceful contact had dislodged some papers from the inside pocket of Daniel's jacket. As he bent to retrieve them one of them became separated from the others. It was a letter, Christa realised, the paper headed with the name of one of the country's most prestigious universities.

Frowning, she stared at it and then, before Daniel could stop her, she bent down and picked it up, reading it quickly before he could retrieve it from her, her face pale with shock as she stared at him.

'You've applied to go back to lecturing,' she said in disbelief. 'But you said that that was something you would never do.'

'Yes,' Daniel agreed quietly.

'Then why?' Christa asked him, even though she suspected she already knew the answer.

'Because you mean more to me than the centre does, Christa, and I could see that it was always going to come between us, that while it existed you would always have fears and doubts.'

'No, Daniel. No,' Christa protested. She felt as though he had held a mirror up to her soul and shown her how mean and selfish she had been.

'Oh, no. You mustn't do that,' she told him fiercely. 'You mustn't.'

Christa saw from the look in his eyes that she hadn't convinced him.

Taking a deep breath and then crossing her fingers behind her back for good measure, she said quickly, 'You *can't* do it. It wouldn't be fair. A baby... a child needs fresh air and freedom...not...not the cloistered atmosphere of a university.

'He or she needs a father who will be there for him, not one who's too busy lecturing or constantly away on lecture tours.'

'A baby...' Daniel had gone oddly pale. 'Are you sure?' he demanded.

'No,' Christa admitted honestly. 'But...but sooner or later there *will* be a baby, Daniel...a child...our child. Won't there?'

'Yes,' he told her thickly. 'Yes. Yes... Yes... Oh, God, Christa what the hell are we doing here? Let's go home...'

Two hours later, curled up next to him in the chair in her workroom, the samples she had brought home with her scattered all over the floor, Christa sighed happily and snuggled closer to him.

'You've never asked me what exactly I did say to the Chamber of Commerce head,' Daniel reminded her.

'I didn't need to,' Christa responded. 'It isn't important...'

'Mmm...perhaps not, but, just for the record, what I actually told him was that, in view of the personal relationship which had developed between us, I wanted to put on record that my challenge to you and my claim to the chamber was null and void.

'It was the honourable thing to do,' he added, when Christa looked lovingly at him.

'Like marrying me because I might be carrying your child?' she teased him, her lips touching his.

'No, not at all like that,' he laughed. 'That is extremely dishonourable, given the fact that, if I'm honest, I've been secretly praying that you have conceived.'

'And if I haven't?' Christa asked him.

His mouth against hers, Daniel told her lovingly, 'Well then, in that case, we'll just have to try harder, won't we, my love?'

Christa's response was non-vocal, but abundantly plain nevertheless.

Coming Next Month

HARLEQUIN PRESENTS®

THE BEST HAS JUST GOTTEN BETTER!

#1845 RELATIVE SINS Anne Mather
Alex mustn't know Sara's secret. But her small son Ben adores him and she has to admit that Alex is ideal father material.... Is the answer to keep it in the family?

#1846 ANGRY DESIRE Charlotte Lamb
(SINS)
Gabriella realized she couldn't marry Stephen and ran out on him on their wedding day. But Stephen wouldn't take "I don't" for an answer....

#1847 RECKLESS CONDUCT Susan Napier
(9 to 5)
Marcus Fox didn't approve of Harriet. She put it down to her new bubbly blond image. Then Marcus reminded her of the events at the last office party....

#1848 THEIR WEDDING DAY Emma Darcy
(This Time, Forever)
Once he was her boss, and her lover.... And now Keir is back in Rowena's life. Can they let go of their past and forge a future together?

#1849 A KISS TO REMEMBER Miranda Lee
(Affairs to Remember)
It was time for Angie to stop comparing every man she met with Lance Sterling and move on. Here she was, twenty-four and a virgin...and suddenly Lance was back in her life!

#1850 FORSAKING ALL OTHERS Susanne McCarthy
When Leo Ratcliffe proposed to Maddie, was he promising the true love of which she'd always dreamed—or merely offering a marriage for his convenience?

HARLEQUIN PRESENTS®

Dear Reader,

re: RECKLESS CONDUCT by Susan Napier
Harlequin Presents #1847

Harriet had decided to change her whole image, but Marcus Fox, chairman of the company she worked for, didn't approve....

Yours faithfully,

The Editor

P.S. Harlequin Presents—the best has just gotten better! Available in November wherever Harlequin books are sold.

P.P.S. Look us up on-line at: http://www.romance.net

Harlequin brings you the best books, by the best authors!

ANNE MATHER

"...her own special brand of enchantment."
—*Affaire de Coeur*

Watch for:
#1845 RELATIVE SINS
by Anne Mather

Sara has a secret that her brother-in-law, Alex, must
never know. But her small son, Ben, adores him. Sara
has to admit that Alex is ideal father material, but his
motives are a mystery to her. Is he playing a game to
which only he knows the rules?

Harlequin Presents—the best has just gotten better!
Available in November wherever
Harlequin books are sold.

Look us up on-line at: http://www.romance.net

HARLEQUIN ◆ PRESENTS®

TAUTH-14